Monterey Bay 1960:
Lady of Cannery Row

Glen Watson

ISBN:0615633730
ISBN-13:9780615633732

DEDICATION

To my wife, Marg, my brothers, George and Gordon, and my Salinas friends and diving buddies, Carl Clark, Jerry Cole, and Jim Hunter, who made a small town Montana boy feel right at home in Salinas. And in memory of Jim Hunter, who died much too young.

The Fire

It's strange what triggers a chain of events, or I guess destiny might be a more appropriate term. And it's not unusual for a destiny to be triggered by a catastrophe that at the time seems so tragic that one may never recover from it. But maybe it takes a catastrophe to set in motion something that is meant to be. It was the fifteenth of November 1954, and Saco, pretty much like the rest of the state of Montana, was well into winter. Harvey, a mechanic, had been working at the International Harvester Agency for about a year and doing an okay job when he was sober. And he may well have been sober on the day he was draining gasoline from a tractor that was parked inside the garage. Harvey didn't know how much gasoline was in the tractor's gas tank he was draining into a container, but soon found there was more than what the container would hold as the gasoline started overflowing and running across the concrete floor to the pilot light on the natural gas heater that attempted to keep the garage warm. Harvey, in a surprisingly apathetic voice said, "Ralph, we've got problem in here." The flowing gasoline didn't hesitate to ignite, and within minutes an entire wall of the garage was engulfed in flames. And within a few hours, the raging fire had burned the entire business to the ground. It burned so quickly, and was so hot, that Saco's volunteer fire department, using the small town's nearly antique fire truck, elected to keep the buildings near the burning business cool to prevent an entire block from going down. And the determined volunteers also stayed their distance from the burning buildings, and rightly so, for the hardware store connected to the garage contained thousands of rounds of ammunition.

Though the Murray's International Harvester agency, with the hardware store and garage, had been the largest business in Saco, like many businesses, if there were any profits, most of it went back into the business. The majority of the people that lived in Phillips County, where Saco is located, were poor. And the Murray family felt quite comfortable among the poor, since they too were poor. Yet, the two younger Murray boys didn't have much time to think about being poor, with school, odd jobs, and helping out in the business, and the oldest Murray boy, almost into high school, spent his summers working as a hired hand on a forty thousand-acre wheat farm just out of Saco and winters working with his dad.

The fire devastated the boys' mom and dad, for their dream had been shattered within hours, after years of working toward it. None of the family was happy about having to move back to Glasgow where they owned an old house that only had two small bedrooms and one bath. The second bedroom and bath with indoor plumbing had been added to the original structure. An outhouse was still standing in the backyard, but had become a storage area. But at least the house was a place to live and their dad could restart the previous automotive repair shop he ran.

Return to Glasgow

Glasgow, a town about forty miles east of Saco, is just off Highway 2, a narrow two-lane highway that runs all the way across the state of Montana. Alongside this frequently treacherous highway, numerous white metal posts, some with a single cross indicating one death, and some with numerous crosses indicating several deaths, are a reminder that Highway 2 is not always a forgiving road. Glasgow, by Montana standards, could be called a city, since it boasted a population of over two thousand. When the family returned to Glasgow, their dad reopened his previous business. But within a year, even that business was interrupted, not by a catastrophe like the fire, but by a visit of an old friend that lived in California. He asked their dad if he would consider moving to California for a government job at Fort Ord, an Army base located between Monterey and Salinas. The base needed a good mechanic quite badly, and the boys' dad, without exaggeration, was most likely one of the top mechanics in Montana, and kept up with the latest automotive technology, which was becoming quite complex. Cars in the late fifties were beginning to have more sophisticated electronic systems, one of which was the torsion leveling on the 1955 Packard. The purpose of the system was to keep the car level regardless of where weight was added. If you loaded the Packard's trunk down with a lot of luggage or had several passengers in the backseat, the system would automatically level the car. However, none of the mechanics at the Packard dealer knew how to repair the system and they called upon the boys' dad to repair an irate customer's new Packard that had its rear bumper nearly dragging on the ground. The customer was threatening to return the Packard and buy a Chevy. The boys' dad studied the torsion leveling schematics to determine how the system worked, repaired it, and the customer drove off with a smile on his face and a cigar in his mouth. If you were a Packard buyer, you generally had some money or at least pretended you did.

The boys' dad reluctantly agreed to take the job in California. He knew that it was the best thing for the family, but they knew it was difficult for him to give up his independence of having his own business, hunting, and lifelong friends. He was a pioneer, a thinker, inventor, and thrived on being part of new technology, but moving to California and working for the government was not a good fit, but Fort Ord was getting a heck of mechanic.

Back Porch Recollections

Fourteen-year old Robert Murray had just come from inside the house and is balancing a scuba tank that is resting on the back porch with one hand, and holding his model 94 Winchester rifle with the other. If he could only take two items with him, these be would his choice. Though the back porch where Robert was standing was rather crude, since it was made of six four-by-fours resting directly on the ground, it matched the house, for the house had no formal foundation either, except for some haphazardly placed large rocks. He looks at the backyard with the dilapidated garage, an old outhouse and the muddy alley and suddenly it came over him that the shabby yard and old buildings, that he had previously felt embarrassed about, were actually full of fantastic memories. This yard, a testing area for ideas, had provided years of projects and adventures, some worked and some didn't, but what a great way to grow up, having a place like this as a testing grounds with no adult intervention. There never seemed to be any restrictions on what they could in this yard. He knew there were no other parents who would have tolerated the projects and messes that they created here. He looked at the shabby roof of the garage and remembered the day they found the valuable ten foot long wooden shipping crate in the back alley of the furniture store. When he and his younger brother found this treasure, he stood guard, while the younger brother ran home to get the older brother so they could carry the monstrous crate home. Initially the crate was a military aircraft that they decked out with a washing machine agitator for a prop, two seats, control stick, a gas gauge, windshield, and a broom stick on a swivel for a machine gun. This airplane was part of the yard for several weeks and getting plenty of combat flight time, until they suddenly had an idea to make it into a lookout tower by erecting it on top of the garage. It was a three step operation, consisting of first getting it on top the garage, then tipping it on end and then figuring out a way to keep it from toppling over. And somehow, no one was injured in the precarious evolution. The younger brother, being the smallest and lightest was the first to try out the ladder they built inside the crate. He wasted no time scurrying up the ladder and becoming the first lookout.

And then Robert turns and looks at the rickety screen door of their house with the peeling paint and realizes a similarity between the house and the yard. It wasn't a fancy house, to say the least, but it was a great home. Just as the boys turned the shabby yard into a wonderful place to grow up, their mom turned the not so great house into a wonderful home. And as he thought of it as great home, he smiled because the memories of Christmas, which was always a favorite time, came to him. It was always the boys' responsibility to get the Christmas tree from the downtown tree lot. All of the trees were the same price, so it made sense to get the biggest one, so big that it required all three of them to carry it home. But, a ten foot tree in a house that had a seven foot ceiling, well, that was a problem, but quickly solved with a saw. It didn't take them long to realize they should have cut the section from the base of the tree rather than the top. Though the tree looked kind of weird that year, their mom and dad said nothing about it.

Robert's face has taken on a trance like appearance, and feels as though he is reviewing the first phase of his life and just now, as his two brothers are standing next to a loaded half-ton pickup truck that is parked behind their house, he realizes the huge part they had played in his life.

Then he wondered why he was thinking of them as being in the past, for they were all going to California, but he had the feeling that each would be going their separate ways when they reached their destination. On one hand he felt sad because it would change the relationship with each other, but on the other hand, he was being cut free of them, forcing him to become more independent and responsible for the next phase of his life. And maybe he no longer needed the crutch they had provided. It's as though he is getting a brand new start, almost as though he will become different person. As he thought about it, maybe he had started to break from the dependency of his brothers when he began hunting deer and antelope with their dad. Neither of his brothers had interest in that. Oh, his two brothers sometimes went along on hunting trips for ducks and pheasant, but not bigger game. Maybe big game hunting was the point where he was starting to break away from them. Perhaps it was a sample or trial run of independence.

Other than big game hunting, the bond between the boys always came together whenever a project or interest was stimulated like when they were fascinated by flocks of geese that always seemed to be a mile high and on their way to someplace that had a more hospitable climate. The boys weren't interested in shooting the geese, for they all had passed up a chance to shoot at geese with a ten-gauge lever action shotgun that belonged one of their dad's friends. Though the severe kick of the ten-gauge may have influenced their decision to not shoot the shotgun, they really didn't want to kill or injure those high flyers. But they were interested in the challenge of bringing them closer, so they made goose decoys out of sheets of cardboard and used wax crayons to color and protect the cardboard from the weather. Though they never lured any geese, it didn't discourage them from moving on to other projects. They were always building, fixing, or creating something for they had been a team that never gave up doing and trying.

But of all of the family members, it was Jerry, a small herding dog, who explicitly showed his hunting enthusiasm. He'd go crazy when they got the rifles or shotguns out. Yet, the only thing the brothers had ever witnessed him killing was a chicken now and then, and he was quite proficient at it, but as one might imagine, killing a neighbor's chicken wasn't a good thing. And other dogs, well, let's just say Jerry picked his dog friends carefully, and the German Shepherd, a dog two and a half times his size, that hung out at the Texaco station was not one them. And the boys never did figure out why the paperboy that delivered papers to a neighbor's house kept bringing his dog around, because, well, Jerry just wasn't fond of that dog either. Keeping Jerry out of trouble was sometimes difficult, but just as the brothers watched out for each other, they watched out for Jerry, for he was one of them. Thinking back on it, perhaps Jerry didn't have an interest in establishing dog friends because of his close bond with the boys.

Robert, still standing on the porch, watches the older brother walk around to the tailgate of the truck and starts rearranging a few items so they will be easily accessible during the trip. The items included three flour sacks that the boys' mom would have normally made into dishtowels or pillowcases. But for this occasion, these versatile sacks were luggage, each containing a change of clothes and a toothbrush. The flower sacks are sitting on the lowered tailgate alongside a case of Great Falls Select Beer. The younger brother is holding two facemasks and two snorkels.

The older brother said, "Where you gonna put those?"

"With our clothes, thought we might get a chance to use them at the motel. Some motels have swimming pools."

The older brother nodded and smiled, "Yeah, maybe so. You know, you guys are gonna grow fins and gills with the amount of time you spend underwater." The younger brother smiles as he puts the facemasks and snorkels in the flour sacks. They were going to stay at a motel for two nights during their trip, and even though they had never stayed in a motel before, they had seen pictures in magazines and movies showing that some motels had swimming pools, and they just wanted to be ready in case. Though the facemasks and snorkels were important to the younger brothers, the older brother was more concerned about the case of beer.

He had gotten into the routine of having a couple beers each evening, a ritual he had picked up at the age of fifteen when he spent his summers as a hired hand on the Saco wheat farm. It was one of the benefits or perhaps breaks from the arduous fourteen-hour, seven day a week summer job. Being only nineteen now, he knew he would not be able to buy beer along the way. No, he couldn't buy it legally in Montana either, but one of the guys at the Texaco station, where he had been working since the family moved back to Glasgow would always get it for him. The Texaco station job was nearly as grueling as his farm job considering the extreme weather conditions. It was quite common for him to change large truck tires outside when winter temperatures were often minus thirty degrees and several times would drop as far as minus fifty. And the summer temperatures often exceeded a hundred. There were few easy jobs in Northeastern Montana. Despite the weather conditions and few good job opportunities, the older brother was not happy about his family moving from Montana.

As Robert stood watching his older brother arrange the flower sacks, he smiled, for they reminded him of Janet, a girl that he started first grade with. No, it wasn't that she looked like a flour sack. No, she was a pretty girl. It's just that the flour sacks reminded him of the bread his mom made, and triggered a memory of an incident that took place when they were in third grade together. It was a Friday just before Christmas vacation was to start, and they were having a Christmas party at school, which meant the students ate lunches they brought from home in the classroom. Robert opened his paper lunch bag that had been used and reused and refolded so often that you could see the individual fibers that made up the bag. The worn bag contained a cheese sandwich on homemade bread, half an apple, and a homemade oatmeal cookie. Janet approached Robert and said, "My mom packed me a baloney sandwich. I can't eat meat on Fridays because I'm Catholic. I wondered if you'd like to trade sandwiches. Does your sandwich have meat on it?"

Though only in the third grade, Robert knew the Catholic rule about not eating meat on Fridays, but he didn't know that Janet was a Catholic. She didn't act like a Catholic. Most of the Catholic kids he knew, the boys anyway, were jerks. Well, there were a few that were okay. But regardless of the reason, he was glad she didn't go to Catholic school. But still, it seemed strange that her mom would forget the meat rule, a rule that even he knew, and he wasn't even a Catholic. Robert found himself in an embarrassing situation, his sandwich was not meat, but it was made with homemade bread, and he associated homemade bread with being poor. He didn't want Janet to know his family ate homemade bread, so he lied to her and said, "No, its meat." And normally, it would have been ground venison, but his mom was out of Miracle Whip.

He remembered Janet smiling and then she said, "Well, I don't think one sandwich will matter." And then she started walking back to her desk, but did turn and smile again before continuing. He liked that, and he was particularly pleased that she didn't ask anyone else to trade. And just now, as he was thinking about the incident, he realized that Janet had made the sandwich herself. He smiled and laughed a little, shook his head in disgust and realized how stupid he was. He would miss her, even though he was still too shy to talk to her very much. Well, he thought, at least I got to walk home from school a few times with her.

But the memory of walking home with Janet somehow triggered another incident that was not as pleasant. He was walking home with Jimmy, a kid that he almost considered sort of a friend. Not somebody he hung out with, but he always seemed like an okay kid. Well, the last time he spoke or walked with Jimmy was when Jimmy made the remark about their house. The hurtful remark caused tears to form in Robert's eyes, and he immediately headed to the other side of the street and started thinking that maybe Jimmy was a damn Catholic, even if he didn't go Catholic school. He tried to put the incident out of his mind, but the remark still lingered. But now the thoughts no longer generated tears. Nope, no tears just anger. He looked down at his hand that was holding the rifle and saw that it was clenched so tightly around the rifle stock that his fingers had turned white. His hand seemed to have clenched without his knowledge. He forced the situation out his mind by switching back to Janet and convinced that she wasn't a Catholic.

He had several friends when they lived in Saco, but in Glasgow, the only kid he considered a good friend was Orville, whose family was equally or most likely, more poor than his family. And thinking of Orville reminded him of the kayak incident on the slough. The two of them had built several kayaks using willows connected together with copper wire that they salvaged from worn out automobile starters and generators. Once the frame of willows was built, they covered it with canvas. And they were getting pretty good at building the kayaks. Not that they would have ever have placed an advertisement in the back of a "Popular Science" magazine, similar to the Chris-Craft's advertisement, which Robert was very familiar with. He had even sent in one of those coupons you cut out for free additional information which came in the mail within a month. However, the coupon also generated a visitor who came by car about six months later. It seems that a Chris-Craft salesman was making his way across Montana and stopped by to make contact with an interested and potential customer. Yet it seemed odd, after seeing their house that the salesman, who was selling boats that could easily have cost more than the Murray's entire house, still went to the rickety screen door, knocked and asked for Mr. Robert Murray. Robert's dad answered the door, held back a grin, pointed and said, "There he is. He's the one playing with the dog on the grass."

The salesman looked at the young boy, smiled and said, "Well, you folks have a nice day."

Usually they tested the kayaks in the Milk River, but the last one they built, they took to the slough that was about a mile out of town. They had removed their shoes and put them in the kayak because they had to wade through the muddy bank, to get the kayak into deep enough water before getting in. Finally, they were paddling in the middle of the slough when Orville started goofing around, rocking the kayak, and it capsized, throwing both of them into the water. The water was like mud soup, with absolutely no visibility, and the bottom was more of the same, but thicker. Fortunately, they didn't have to swim because they were able to stand on the bottom to upright the kayak. However, the situation wasn't helped by a very young kid that lived near the slough yelling from the bank, "My mom said you're gonna catch polio." This was a couple of years before polio vaccine was available, but it was well known that polio could be contacted through dirty water, and that slough was, without a doubt, dirty water. Both Robert and Orville knew the kid was probably right, but polio, was not their primary concern at the time. Though Robert had retrieved both of his shoes and one of Orville's, his other shoe was on the bottom, somewhere. They used their bare feet to search for the missing shoe. For nearly an hour they searched with no luck. For both of the boys, losing a shoe was as serious as catching polio, for neither of them had an extra pair.

As Robert lingered on the porch with his rifle and scuba tank, his view of the truck, loaded with what appeared to be mostly junk, and his two brothers standing next to it was a pathetic sight. Yet, for some reason the spotlight mounted on the roof of the truck was bothering him even more. Probably because he couldn't fix the entire image, but there was something he could do about that spotlight that looked out of place. The farmer who previously owned the truck used the spotlight for hunting jackrabbits at night. If you shine a spotlight on a rabbit at night, the rabbit will stay perfectly still. Technically, they weren't rabbits, but hares, because their fur changed from brown to white in the winter, whereas rabbit's fur does not change color. But everybody called them jackrabbits. The farmer did not hunt these jackrabbits for the sport. He hunted them for the two or three dollars that he could get for each thick white winter coat. Though the spotlight previously had a function, now it just looked out of place. Robert didn't have any illusion that removing that spotlight would do much to change the overall image, but he felt obligated to try something. He picked up the scuba tank with one hand and the rifle with the other and walked from the porch to the truck. Still holding the neck of the scuba tank, he let the bottom rest on the ground and then handed the rifle to his older brother and said, "Here's the tank and the last rifle. Be okay if I take off that spotlight?"

His older brother with a surprised look said, "What brought that up?"

"I don't know. Just looks kinda funny."

His older brother laughs and said, "Well, it sure matches our luggage."

Robert nods, laughs and said, "Yeah."

"When you take it off, make sure you tape up those wires so they don't short out. And fill the holes with some solder in case it rains."

His younger brother said, "Where's Jerry gonna sit?" Jerry heard his name and walked over to the boys, sat down at their feet, and looked curiously up at them.

His older brother said, "On the floor board I guess. Be kinda crowded down there. At least he can get air from the vent." The truck had a vent opening on the hood near the windshield operated by a lever inside the cab.

Though the lives of all four of them would change when they reached their destination, it would be Jerry's life that would be completely turned upside down. But for now, Jerry was just happy to be going along for he was always with the boys. Even when they went off to school, he knew when they were coming home and would go down to the corner and wait for them. Jerry had never been restricted by fences or ordinances, nor was he familiar with an institution called animal control, that the boys knew as a dogcatcher, something that they had only seen in the movies. The movies were about the only place that Jerry didn't get to go. Of all the places he went, his favorite was the Public Drug Store on Main Street where they had those really thick milk shakes that came with a glass filled to the brim and dripping over the side a bit, and the frosty metal container that contained another half a glass. Jerry knew he wasn't suppose to go into places like the grocery store or post office, but from previous experience, the drug store was one place that it was okay to go into when the time was right. He didn't go in when the boys went in. Initially, he sat outside the drugstore and waited. Well, he waited until the next customer opened the door and he'd sneak in and scurry toward the booth where the boys were sitting. The druggist probably never knew of Jerry's routine and Mary Ann, the waitress, chose to ignore him among the boys' legs under the booth and automatically brought a small bowl with the milkshakes, a trick she quickly learned to prevent having to clean up a sticky mess under the booth where the boys had been giving Jerry his share of the chocolate milkshakes.

Traveling West

So, no one could speak for Jerry, even though he must have been very uncomfortable down on the floorboard of the truck, among the three pair of legs and shoes, while his damp nose tried to salvage some fresh air from the opened hood vent. But he didn't whine about it. No, he was no whiner. He was just content be included in the trip. Those who didn't know the

Murray family very well, and perhaps didn't care to know them, always thought Jerry was merely another Murray kid.

Robert was happy to be moving. Even though he did not know what to expect, the trip was giving him a lot of time to think as he rode along in the truck and sometimes taking over the driving when his older brother was tired. He determined that life would be different and it would be better, but he had no way of knowing how much better, until his first trip to Monterey Bay.

The older brother hadn't said much during the trip, but at one point he did say, "I guess Dad started working at that Army base. That's what Mom said when she called last. You know, Dad didn't want to move out there. And I don't think I'm gonna like it."

Robert said, "Why's that?"

"I don't know. I just like Montana."

His younger brother said, "How many motels we staying in?"

His older brother said, "Two, unless the truck breaks down. Course then we'd probably just camp out if it's more than two."

His younger brother asked, "They have swimming pools?"

"I don't know."

His younger brother asked, "Jerry going to have to sleep in the truck?"

Robert said, "No, he'll be with us."

"Thought they didn't allow dogs in motels."

"Jerry's not a regular dog. He's gonna be with us in the room. Maybe we can put some of those dark glasses on him. Like those Hollywood people wear."

His younger brother laughs and said, "Yeah."

The truck engine strained a bit while pulling up the mountain grades as they traveled west, forcing the driver to go out of overdrive, or sometimes shifting the three-speed on the column to second gear, but they had been making good time since they left Glasgow. Both the engine and transmission were strong and doing their job despite that the 1954 International R100 was nearly loaded to the top of the sturdy homemade wooden side rails that the boys had built. The load consisted of things that most people would have thought of as junk that should have been on its way to the dump ground. But none of the passengers sitting in the half-ton International Harvester truck thought of it as junk. The load was covered with an oil-impregnated tarp, oil that never seemed to dry and stained your hands and clothes and continued to emit a strong odor for the life of the tarp. Under the tarp was a black and white television set, which was probably the only visible item that would be of obvious value to an unimaginative person, even though color television had been available for about four years or so. Some might wonder why anyone would haul things like twenty-five feet of lead water pipe that the boys salvaged when Glasgow replaced the lead pipes with galvanized pipe. No, it wasn't replaced because of a lead health hazard. It was replaced because the inside diameter of the ancient lead pipes had become so small from being flattened by the pressure of the heavy earth, and from calcium buildup, that the pipes no longer supplied an adequate amount of water to the houses on the south side of town. This valuable lead pipe would have ended up at the county dump if the young boys hadn't had the foresight to salvage it. But hidden among, what appeared to be worn out household items was the scuba tank and regulator, carefully packed between army surplus blankets. The scuba tank was treated with as much respect as the 25-35 Winchester lever-action rifle, 32 Winchester special lever-action rifle, 22 single-shot Winchester rifle, 22 automatic Winchester rifle, 20-gauge Montgomery Wards pump shotgun and a 410 single-shot Winchester shotgun. The boys knew that the scuba tank could be as deadly as the guns if the valve on the end of the tank had broken off and released the 2,700 pounds of air pressure inside. With that much pressure, the tank had the capability of turning into a missile that could penetrate car sheet metal. Of course the tank only had about 500 pounds of pressure to keep the moisture out, but just as the guns were always treated as being loaded, a rule that the boys adhered to since they able to walk, the scuba tank was always treated as being fully charged. Now, having a few guns in Northeastern Montana, well anywhere in Montana, is quite normal. Many of the poor families, who really never recovered from the depression of the thirties, or may not have even recognized there was a depression, because they had always been depressed since the homestead days, used guns for hunting food. Well, the 25-35 and 32 Winchester special and the shotguns were for hunting, but the twenty-two rifles were more like training devices. The passengers in the truck had shifted from their Daisy air rifles to twenty-two rifles at about the age of nine or ten, which was quite common in Montana. For many, hunting in Montana was much more than a sport. Although, the cattle ranchers and the wealthier people in town had a consistent diet of beef, the boys' family relied on venison, antelope, mallard ducks, pheasant, grouse, and sage hen for their meat supply. Although guns were common, scuba equipment in Northeastern Montana was not considered a typical household item. In fact, if a Montana Highway Patrolman had pulled them over for some reason and had seen the guns, beer, and scuba equipment, he more than likely would have said, "What the hell you boys doing with that underwater stuff?"

Believe it or not, Northeastern Montana was never mentioned in "Skin Diver", the first diving magazine that was published in the United States. The boys still had the very first issue that had been published in 1951, though it was in no condition to be a collector's item, for it had been read and reread so many times that the stapled binding was covered with yellowed Scotch tape. Nope, Northeastern Montana was not considered a scuba diving Mecca. And it is believed by some, that the only time that Northeastern Montana was ever favorably mentioned about anything was when the United States Government, being lobbied by Jim Hill of the Great Northern Railroad fame, was trying to attract homesteaders to settle in the area. Apparently, none of the Government officials that described Northeastern Montana in the "Homesteaders Guide to a Better Life," had actually had set foot in Montana. But Jim Hill and his railroaders had been there, and they knew better than to offer more than the free one-way ticket, normally costing twelve dollars and fifty cents, to attract settlers from the East. If the eastern settlers had been in possession of a return ticket, most would not have stayed the night. And Lewis and Clark only spent as much time in this part of Montana as it took to scurry along the Missouri River as they were being attacked, not by savage Indians, but by extreme cold, extreme heat, and the largest mosquitoes known to mankind.

Robert and his younger brother had ordered their Squale facemasks several years ago through an advertisement in “Skin Diver” magazine. Selecting the French made facemask was not a difficult decision because there weren’t that many choices, but it was a quality mask with shatterproof glass. Yet, spending four dollars and ninety five cents for each mask was not taken lightly because it was hard earned money from lawn cutting, storm window installation, pin setting at the bowling alley, paper route, and rotary tiller business. Any purchases the boys made were carefully calculated. However, when they ordered the masks, what they had not taken into consideration was that Chester Tattle, who controlled the swimming pool, civic center and park, had illogical, unbending rules, and was a long time enemy of the boys. It seemed to the boys that Chester had a serious obsession of trying to keep them from playing ball at the park. This is not the time to go into great detail about Chester. You just need to know that he was no friend to the boys. The boys’ intention was that the masks would be particularly useful in the Glasgow swimming pool, where they spent a lot of time during the summer months when the temperature was consistently pushing a hundred degrees. But Chester had a rule that no glass items could be brought into the swimming pool. The boys were young, but they very astute and understood the corruption of city government. It was apparent to the boys that Chester was getting a kickback from the local Dime Store that only sold the useless little kid’s facemasks that had plastic lenses that fogged over even if you rubbed spit in them every dive. Fortunately the boys were able to bypass Chester and go directly to the lifeguard with documentation that described the glass in the masks as shatterproof and virtually unbreakable down to one thousand feet. Well, maybe the thousand feet was an exaggeration, and the depth didn’t really have anything to do with breakage, but it seemed to be a good selling point. The lifeguard, a very attractive high school girl, was not as fond of Chester, as he was of her and she had no objection to breaking some of his rules to get even with his gropes and leers, which she tolerated because she needed the job.

The boys spent most their summers from one to three o'clock in the deep end of the pool practicing snorkeling and building up their lung capacity while watching the images of the other swimmers, divers, and jumpers. Since the pool water was not filtered, you could not stand on the side of the pool and see the bottom. Since you could not see the bottom of the pool, when you went swimming there, you had to have a pool buddy. Every half-hour the lifeguard would blow her whistle and everybody would have to get out of the pool with his or her buddy. If somebody's buddy was missing, it would be assumed that he or she was probably at the bottom of the pool somewhere or in the bathroom. Even though the water was not filtered, or heated and seldom reached more than fifty-five degrees, it was still safer than swimming in the Milk River that was the recipient of Glasgow's sewage and the sewage of other towns along the river. But swimming in the Milk River was more interesting because of the rope swing that hung from a large tree limb overhanging the river, which got its fair share of use by the boys and their friends. Robert had always heard the rumor that girls would hide in the bushes near the river and watch the naked boys swim, but he'd never seen any girls lurking in the bushes. They had to swim naked since they weren't allowed to swim in the river. And coming home with wet swimsuits when the pool wasn't open would cause their parents unnecessary worry.

Beverly, the lifeguard, became quite familiar with the boys. She would often kneel down on the side of the pool, lean over and watch the young divers begin their descent into the murky water toward the bottom. She was impressed by their gracefulness as they tucked into a ball and flipped their legs up toward the surface, while using their hands to propel down until their feet were completely submerged before they started kicking toward the bottom. Each dive was a textbook dive that they had learned from "Skin Diver" magazine. Since the pool visibility was limited, within seconds they were no longer visible and that bothered her for about a week. If something happened to them, Chester would surely blame her because she let those trouble-making little bastards in with glass facemasks. She soon stopped worrying about them and became fascinated by their continually longer time underwater. And the young divers, though only in grade school, were quite aware of her too, for Beverly had some cleavage. But I'm sure they didn't have the appreciation for her cleavage that Chester had. But cleavage for the two boys was merely a side benefit. What they really appreciated was that Beverly, who they considered well toward becoming an adult, treated them with respect and didn't try to manage their lives like many adults that are in charge of kids.

The boys' independence showed, for they never bothered to join the Boy Scouts or play team sports. If they played baseball or basketball they put together their own team and played when they wanted to play. And besides, Jerry liked playing too. In fact, he could catch a high fly ball and was great at picking up speedy grounders. The boys readily accepted the supervision of their parents and teachers, but they didn't have time to take on additional adult supervision from needy adults. They had jobs, and things to invent, and things to build. The boys had the impression that certain men become leaders of kids because it makes them feel important to be able to order somebody around, under the premise that it builds morality, character, and teamwork. They had already learned morality from their parents and teachers and their character was developing as they dreamed up new ideas for projects. Whether it was building kayaks or erecting a shipping container on top of the garage. Each project was always a team effort that was successfully handled without adult supervision. They even performed their own first aid as long at the injury wasn't too serious. One day they were working on a project in the backyard and Billy, a younger neighbor, was watching and happened to step on a nail that protruded from a board. Billy started crying and his initial reaction was to head for home, but as he started running it was as though he had a ski attached to his foot, so he didn't get very far. To keep the panic from reaching Billy's mom, the boys were able remove the board, take his shoe off and treat the small wound with peroxide and then apply a piece of masking tape to the puncture and he was just fine. Much of their medical training was gained from taking care of Jerry, for it wasn't unusual for him to come home from a night romp with porcupine needles protruding from his nose, a torn ear, swollen eye, or thorn in his paw.

Glasgow had what they called a Huckleberry Finn parade where the adults built floats for the kids and dressed the kids up in the Huckleberry Finn theme. Mrs. Kattell, the boys' neighbor, who was several years over seventy or maybe closer to eighty, and often asked the boys to do odd jobs, was always watching them build things like kayaks and soap box cars and igloos in the winter. She told the boys' mom that she didn't have to go to that parade because every day she watched the real Huckleberry Finns from her window. And of course the boys didn't even bother to walk downtown to watch the adult-built floats, adult-sewn or adult-purchased Huckleberry Finn clothes. The boys had real patches, sewn on top of real holes in all of their jeans. The boys' jeans were often hand-me downs from a cousin whose parents moved from Montana to Portland, Oregon during the depression. Since he was an only child, the clothes that came from him were just a little faded and never had holes in the knees. The oldest boy got the jeans from Portland first and by the time the next boy in line got them, they generally had a patch on each knee.

Salinas, California

Salinas, with its mild climate and prime farm land, is known as the lettuce capital of the world, and this land also grows celery and most everything else that someone would want in a salad. And Salinas is also well known as John Steinbeck's birthplace. The boys' parents initially rented a small house in an older section of Salinas until they discovered a contractor was building new houses in South Salinas that were within walking distance to the schools that boys would be attending and easy access for their dad's commute to Fort Ord. In this South Salinas area they found a brand new house that they could get into if they took out a thirty year loan, but taking on a thirty year loan, that he might not live to pay off, is a scary thought to the boys' dad. Yet, it was cheaper to buy than rent, and as a Navy Seabee in World War II, he was eligible for a GI Bill loan that he had never used. Things seemed to be falling into place for the family, and the boys' mom was elated to move into a new three bedroom house with two baths. The baths had real door knobs rather than an empty thread spool and one bath even had a shower, rather than a very old dinky bathtub. Hardwood covered the floors in all of the rooms rather than worn linoleum and the kitchen cabinets had doors rather than curtains. And the house even had an attached two car garage. Even the location of the house, being within a block of the lettuce fields, gave the area a small touch of country to ease into what would be a large city in Montana. Within fifteen minutes, Robert and his younger brother could be in the country and on their way to the Salinas River. Of course, they were surprised the first time they walked to the river because it had very little water in it. Later they found out that it was an underground river. What the boys didn't know was that a fellow named John Steinbeck walked this area when he was a boy. And it took the boys several trips down Central Avenue to the "Green Frog," a grocery store that was within walking distance from their new house, to discover they had been walking right by the house that John Steinbeck lived in as a boy. Seemed like this Steinbeck thing kept brushing them in the face without them even realizing. Robert had never even heard of the books, "East of Eden", Steinbeck's book about immigrants coming to Salinas or "Cannery Row," a book about the workers and residents of Cannery Row. And it took a couple months before the most valuable thing about Salinas, from the boys' perspective, was to reveal itself, for it was twenty miles to Monterey Bay and the family's only transportation was the 1954 International Harvester pickup truck, that their dad drove to work. And it would be quite sometime later when the vague brush with Steinbeck would take on broader strokes and become much more meaningful to Robert.

Pacific Grove Cove

Pacific Grove, a small community located right along the coast and bordering Monterey, has a place called the Cove. The brothers stood in the parking above the Cove watching three to four-foot waves crash against a concrete wall that was apparently installed to protect the restaurant that perched on a rock ridge above the ocean. The crashing waves could be heard in the parking lot and were impressive, but what really got the boys' attention were the surfers riding surf mats right toward the wall and backing off before they hit the wall. All of the surfers were wearing wetsuits giving an indication that the water was not all that warm. Although the waves were crashing into the wall, the Cove is naturally protected from the open ocean because the terrain comes inland and forms an area similar to a lake. Because of the terrain and the sea wall, the Cove is generally calm and has good visibility. On their second trip to Monterey the brothers brought their army surplus air mattresses, doubled them back and tied them with a rope and were out there riding the surf into the wall. It didn't take long for the boys to realize why most of the surfers wore wetsuits. Despite having no wetsuits, the fifty-five degree water didn't dampen their spirits as they rode the waves. The surfers with the real surf mats appeared to have some respect for the boys, despite the crude flotation devices they were riding, for they braved the cold water without wetsuits. After several rides toward the wall, Robert rested beyond where the waves were breaking and looked down into the fifteen foot deep water. He was astonished by the visibility, which was so good he could see the bottom. And not only that, the rocky bottom was covered starfish, abalone, and sea urchins that he only recognized because he had seen pictures of them in “Skin Diver” magazine. And his excitement continued to grow when a large fish swam from a crevice on the bottom and several smaller fish swam close to his feet and nibbled on his toes. Robert thought that visibility and scenery like this only existed in Bora Bora, Grand Cayman and other famous dive spots that he had seen in “Skin Diver” magazine. His shivering from the icy water seemed be neutralized by thoughts of how many things had happened to allow him to be in this paradise. It was almost as though being in Monterey Bay was something that had been mysteriously planned long before it occurred, and the hours he and his younger brother spent in Fort Peck Lake and the swimming pool with limited visibility and nothing of interest to see was preparation for being here.

Hartnell College Theatre

Robert was extremely nervous as he stood by himself on the stage of the Hartnell College Theater. Drama was an important agenda at Hartnell College, and they had a very nice theatre. The drama instructor was also the speech instructor. As Robert stood behind the podium shaking badly, he looked at the instructor and then scanned the nearly forty freshmen in Speech 101, a required course. This was a new experience to him. Not only public speaking, but the topic he chose revealed things about himself that he wouldn't have admitted when he was younger. It seemed that he stood there for a long time before he heard himself say, "My family moved from Montana two years ago. We lived in two different towns in Northeastern

Montana. The first was Glasgow, a place of a little over two thousand people. We lived there for my first nine years, before moving to Saco, a town of about two hundred and there were another two hundred farmers and ranchers that made up the entire Phillips County where Saco was located."

"I liked Saco, for it seemed like everyone was equally poor and nice. There were a few wealthy people, but none that flaunted their wealth, and I particularly remember a Mr. Woods, who naturally went by the name Timber." Several in the audience laughed and Robert was glad, for it put him more at ease and gave him a chance to catch his breath. Then he continued, "Timber owned thousands of acres of ranch and wheat land, yet despite his wealth, he drove a ten-year old pickup truck and wore an old hat."

"Even though my dad owned an International Harvester business with a hardware store and a repair shop, our family struggled as much as most in town. We couldn't even afford to buy a bike or gun from our own hardware store. But that really didn't bother us because we were always too busy to think about it."

"My younger brother and I delivered groceries for the two grocery stores in Saco. We used wagons to haul foldable wooden grocery boxes. The pay wasn't bad. We got five cents for a small box and ten cents for a large box. And we were also in the theater business." Robert hesitated and looked over the group that now appeared more curious. Then he continued, "Yeah, we were the janitors for the Gem Theatre." Robert waited a few seconds until the laugher stopped, and continued, "We weren't paid a wage, but did have benefits, which were quite generous, for we got into the theater free, saving us fifteen cents a movie. But the best part of going to the movies at the Gem Theater was not the movie, but the girl that took the tickets. She was the theater owner's daughter, Judy, who was a cute girl, the same age as I was, but much more mature, and I could only fantasize that'd she be interested in me. Course at that age, I wouldn't have known what to do with her, nor am I sure I'd know what I'd do with her now." The group laughed. Robert continued, "Judy had one brown eye and one blue eye. Every time I went to the movies she would look at me, smile and jokingly say, 'Where's your ticket?' Believe me, I would have gladly paid the fifteen cents just for that smile and a look at those eyes. And we also worked in our dad's repair shop in our spare time. He didn't pay us, but we learned a lot and it was fun. I mean how many kids get to arc weld, use an acetylene torch, a drill press, a lathe, and a grinder when they are still in grade school. Things were going really well for my family, but they took turn for the worst the day that Saco had the biggest fire the little town had ever known. My dad's business burned to the ground forcing us to move back to Glasgow where we previously lived."

"Glasgow has a north side and a south side with railroad tracks separating the two. We lived on the south side where the older homes were. Now, Glasgow may have been a nice place for many, but for me it was not nice. I had a paper route in Glasgow and each month I had go around collecting the monthly payment for the paper. It seemed that the people that lived in the nicer houses were often the ones that would ask me to come back later because they didn't have change to pay their bill. Oddly, the people that lived in the not so nice houses always seem to have change, and not only that, they were the ones that would invite you in for a cup of hot chocolate during the winter."

"I was getting to an age when wearing patches on my jeans was starting to bother me, but once I got back home, I would sort forget about it. I guess our house was a safe place to be, even though it wasn't a great looking house. But that was something I managed to overlook, for my mom did a good job of making it a comfortable place. But this one day, I was walking home with a kid named Jimmy. We were both thirteen, and I thought he was an okay kid. I had known him since first grade. I never really hung out with him, except for sometimes walking home with him. But this one day, Jimmy said, 'Why do you live in such a shitty house?'" Robert paused for a few seconds and continued, "Him saying that was too much for me. I backed away from him and crossed the street. I didn't want him to see the tears forming in my eyes. That was the last time that I ever talked to Jimmy. After that day, I went out of my way to avoid him. But soon after that incident, something very good happened to me." Robert took a deep breath and continued, "About six months after Jimmy's remark about our house, my dad got a job offer at Fort Ord. They needed a good mechanic. And my dad is one of the best. My family is doing much better since we moved to Salinas and since I've lived here, I've never been treated badly by anybody. And I want you know that I appreciate that." Robert smiled, and continued, "I really do appreciate that."

Then he continued, "You know how you always think of neat things to say after an incident or confrontation with somebody? Well, I wish when Jimmy asked why we lived in such a shitty house, I wished I'd said, you know Jimmy, my dad was just asking me about that last night. My dad wanted to know what I was doing with all of my paper route and odd job money." Though still dabbing their eyes, the group turned to smiles and then laughter.

Hartnell College Psychology 101

Nobody skipped Doctor Healy's psychology class, a required first year course at Hartnell College. Not the good students, bad students, or even football players that had been recruited from as far away as Alaska, Hawaii, and the East Coast, would purposely miss his classes because they were so interesting and entertaining. The combination of his large round head scantly covered with rapidly thinning hair, and eyes covered with very thick glasses made him look exactly like a psychology professor should look. And not only did he look the part, he acted the part. No subject was off limits. And that was his secret. He put on a good show. He was an entertainer, as most successful instructors are, yet had the ability to relate everyday life to psychology, making it interesting, useful, and fascinating. Students did well in his class and had a tremendous amount of respect for him. And the day that Chuck Brandon, a football player, raised his hand and said, "Hey, Doctor Healy, how'd you get such a good lookin' wife?" The entire class was stunned and embarrassed by the intrusive question from who appeared to be an inconsiderate jerk.

Doctor Healy looked at Chuck until his look turned into a stare that lasted long enough to make Chuck squirm, and finally said, "I asked her." The entire class was impressed how well Doctor Healy handled the situation, but entirely disgusted with Chuck Brandon's rudeness.

Diving Buddies

As Robert walked out of the psychology classroom that day, shaking his head about Chuck Brandon's remark, he heard somebody behind him say, "I hear you dive." Robert turned around to the smiling face of a guy who looked exactly as a college student should look with his casual corduroy jacket with leather on the elbows and the horn rimmed glasses. If you were to cast a college student for a movie, you would select this guy. Then he said, "I'm Gary." Robert was surprised, for he remembered Gary from high school, but assumed that Gary didn't know or remember him, for their senior graduating class had over three hundred students. Gary had lived in Salinas all of his life and knew many of the kids in high school, but Robert being a newcomer, understandingly wasn't one of them. But, this Gary guy approaching him seemed to be another example of this friendly town. Gary continued, "I was talking to Ron Malay. He said you dive."

Robert said, "Oh, that's how you knew. Yeah, I snorkel and dive when I have a tank of air. I told Ron I was nearly out of Black Magic and he told me about the dive shop that just opened in Monterey."

"Black Magic, sounds like some kind of voodoo thing."

Robert laughed and said, "It's glue for repairing wetsuits."

"You mean they didn't have a dive shop in Monterey before?"

Robert said, "No, when we started diving in Monterey Bay, the only place to get a tank filled was at a gas station in Pacific Grove where they had a high pressure air compressor, but they didn't have storage bottles, so it would take at least a half hour to fill a tank."

Gary said, "Why so long?"

Robert said, "Well, the gas station compressor put out 3,000 pounds of air but low volume. Whereas, the dive shop has large storage bottles they can fill ahead of time, giving them a large volume of air and can charge a tank in about ten minutes. They just have to keep the tank in water to keep it cool."

Gary said, “The tank heats up?”

Robert said, "Yeah, when you charge the tank, the air compresses and heats up. And when you charge it quickly, it really heats up.”

Gary nods and said, "Boy, there's a lot to learn about this stuff. Who do you dive with?”

“Sometimes my younger brother goes with me, but he doesn’t have a wetsuit and it’s just too cold without one. So usually I go by myself.”

“Sounds like you could use a diving buddy?”

“I hadn't thought about it. You dive?”

“No, but I’ve been reading up on it and thought maybe I could learn with you.”

“I don’t know if I’m qualified to teach anybody to dive.”

Gary said, “Well, how'd you get started?”

“It’s sort of a long story and I’m not a long story kind of guy.” Gary laughed and Robert grinned, thinking that this Gary guy was okay. “Well, it was my older brother. While we were still living in Montana, he ordered a scuba tank and regulator though the mail, but the only place to dive was Fork Peck Lake that had poor visibility and froze over in the winter."

Robert's brother was more interested in the technology of being able to breathe underwater, rather than actually doing it and even getting a scuba tank filled was difficult. His brother worked in a gas station that sold large bottles of welding gases to farmers and the gas station had to order these bottles from a company in North Dakota. So his brother ordered a bottle of three thousand pound purified air from the North Dakota company. But, even with a bottle that large, he could only get a fill and half before the pressure of the scuba tank and large bottle equalized.

“Your brother still dive?"

Robert shook his head and continued, "He used the scuba tank about six times. The last time he used it in Montana, one of his teeth blew up when he was underwater."

"His tooth blew up?"

"Yeah, he was down about ten feet in Fort Peck Lake. At the time he didn't know what happened, but apparently there was an air pocket under a silver filling and breathing the compressed created differential pressure causing the filling to go. That scared my brother. It was the last time he used the scuba equipment in Montana."

"When did you start diving in Monterey Bay?"

"We started snorkeling and then discovered the gas station in Pacific Grove that has the high pressure air compressor. My older brother used the tank once in the Cove but after reading about great white sharks in Monterey Bay, he never went back. So I took over his scuba gear. That was about three years ago."

Gary said, "You know, I've lived in Salinas all my life and I've never been in the ocean. Seems like it's kinda dangerous you diving by yourself. That's what I read, anyway."

"Yeah, I guess. But I like to keep things simple."

Gary smiled and said, "You ever considered diving with somebody?"

"Yeah, I always wanted to dive with Beverly Lamont."

"Beverly Lamont? Who's that?"

"That's a long story."

Gary nodded "Oh, yeah and you're not a long story kinda guy. You drink?"

"Yeah, I like beer."

"Well maybe you can tell me about Beverly sometime over a beer or two."

“Guess I could do that.”

Gary said, “But since you don’t have Beverly as a diving buddy, what do you think about me being your diving buddy?”

Robert smiled, and with a straight face said, “I don’t think you have the breasts for it.” Gary laughed. Robert shrugged and continued, "But I guess we could give it a try."

Gary said, “Where do we start?"

“A swimming pool with facemasks, snorkels, and weight belts so we can work on clearing masks, releasing the weight belts and getting comfortable in the water.”

“Oh, I don’t want to keep adding to the complexity of your life, but I wondered if you'd mind if a buddy of mine joined us. He's pretty much like us, I think. Well, maybe a little more nuts.”

Robert thought about it for while and wondered if he really wanted to be responsible for a second person, but Gary seemed like a nice guy so he said, “Yeah, I guess it'd be okay. But don’t be coming up with some brothers and sisters and half cousins that wanta tag along too.”

Gary laughed and said, “My buddy is going to have to convince his parents that he won’t get eaten by a shark.”

Robert said, "That's what makes diving interesting.” Gary nodded.

Actually, Robert was thinking the real danger of diving Monterey Bay was not the sharks, but the rip tides that could drag you out to sea, the icy cold water that could numb your brain, and the high surf that could beat you up against the rocks. And, in addition to those dangers, an even greater danger of diving Monterey Bay was getting there. At least one or two young men lose their lives each year on the two-lane Monterey Highway. But, he didn’t want to discount the shark hazard because there were sharks, and even great whites. Great whites were sometimes spotted from shore and often seen from fishing boats.

Jim and Gary needed facemasks and snorkels, and weights for the initial training, but Robert suggested they wait on spending a lot of money on weight belts before they really knew if they were serious about diving. He suggested using plastic gallon jugs filled with sand for their pool session. It wasn’t a popular suggestion to either one of them. It seemed that they had some vanity problems, in that the jugs wouldn't give them that Lloyd Bridges, of the popular television show, "Sea Hunt" look. Nor did they seem excited about tying a weighted jug around their waist with a rope that might not be real easy to untie when it was wet. Robert had to admit bringing gallon jugs into the swimming pool might raise some eyebrows and tying the jugs to their waist might make the lifeguard a little uncomfortable. But it was important to have the weight to make swimming more difficult to test their endurance and enable them to stand on the bottom of the pool without fighting to stay down. Jim and Gary seemed optimistic that they were going to become divers so they went ahead and bought the weight belts.

Meeting Nona

Nona, a very attractive shorthaired blond girl, had a puzzled look as the three of them walked toward her carrying diving gear. She said, "Gary and Jim, what are you guys doing here? The kiddy pool is next door." They all laughed. She knew them from high school and Hartnell. As Robert explained to Nona that they wanted to do some dive training in the deep end, he thought she looked familiar and then decided he must have seen her in the student lounge or around campus. Nona smiled and said, “Sounds fine to me, but you guys be careful. I don’t want to get my hair wet.”

Jim and Gary attached their store bought weight belts while Robert put on his homemade army surplus weight belt with homemade lead weights made from the discarded Montana lead water pipe and a homemade brass buckle. Then he slung an army surplus bag around his neck. He didn't notice that Jim and Gary were staring at him until Jim started laughing, but Gary was doing his best to hold a straight face, for he knew exactly what Jim was thinking. And Gary was having a tough time holding back his laughter, because he was thinking that Robert might have a homemade knife attached to the back of that belt. As the two students looked at their instructor, they also saw that Robert's very worn and salt and sun faded blue Squale mask had a black snorkel attached to the strap. The snorkel had several turns of black electrical tape wrapped around the cracked tip.

Jim said, "Wow, you look like a World War II Commando." Robert looked at Jim and Gary with their fancy store-bought weight belts and realized the contrast and broke into a smile and nodded. Robert had never really thought about the contrast of the homemade weight belt and the new commercial belts with the fancy quick release that he had seen in "Skin Diver" magazine advertisements. The contrast reminded him of the homemade wooden rifles that he and his brothers made for playing war. All the kids they played with had store-bought rifles but these kids thought the homemade rifles were really neat and often traded with the boys for the battle of day. Although the commercial belts did have a fancy quick release, Robert thought they might be too easy to accidentally release. If you drop your weight belt while wearing a wetsuit, you will shoot to the surface. A novice may think that a quick trip to the surface is a good thing. But in reality, a quick surface while breathing compressed air, even as shallow as ten feet could injure ones lungs. He had made his buckle, consisting of two parts, by shaping a brass rod and welding the ends together. The end of the web belt snaked around the two-part buckle in a manner that allows releasing with one hand. It was a little more difficult to release than the store bought belts. It had never crossed his mind to drop a belt in the ocean because they take a long time to make and expensive to buy. When the humor faded, Jim and Gary put on their weight belts, grabbed their masks and snorkels and the three of them climbed down the shallow end ladder to the water.

Robert, said, "Don't drop the weight belts on the bottom. They might chip the concrete. Don't want to get her into trouble."

Jim said, "Man, I'd like to get her into trouble." Robert and Gary shook their heads and smiled. Robert liked the humor and was starting to have good feelings about the possibility of the three of them diving together. They swam to the far end of the pool where the water was about ten feet deep and held onto the side.

Robert removed the army surplus bag from around his neck, set it on the pool deck and said, “Put on your facemasks and snorkels and go to the bottom. Then we'll see if you can make it to the surface with the extra weight. Make sure you clear your ears on the way down by yawning or holding your nose and blowing or whatever works." They stood on the pool bottom as a group looking at each other for about ten seconds, and then Robert put his thumb up and they went to the surface and treaded water for several minutes fighting the heavy weight belts that were trying pull them under. Robert said, “Now go back down and wait for me. When I take off my weight belt, you take off yours and gently set it on the bottom. Then we’ll meet on the surface and practice clearing masks." After some practice they were soon proficient at clearing their masks. Robert said, “Now go to the bottom and don’t be surprised if I knock your mask away. Just clear it and come up."

Back on the surface, Robert said, “This is no fun. You guys are making it look too easy. Now let’s go down and put your weight belts on and come back up.”

Robert watched them from the surface and when they picked up their weight belts he dove and picked up his. He realized they should have practiced putting them on before trying it in the water, but after struggling a bit to feed the end of the belt into the buckle, they soon had the belts securely attached to their waists. But you could tell they were ready for a breath of air. They surfaced and Robert grabbed the army surplus bag that he had placed on the pool deck and pulled out three six-inch square slates of white Formica. Each had a line attached. He handed each of them a slate and a grease pencil. “Put these around your neck. We'll be writing notes to each other.”

Jim said, “What do we write?”

“Use your imagination. Come up when you need air." With their weight belts on they quickly sank to the bottom and while standing on the bottom facing each other.

Robert wrote on his slate, “Doing great.”

Gary wrote, “Thanks.”

Jim wrote, “Need air.”

They surfaced for air and he said. “Try it again."

Jim stopped treading water and dropped down immediately as though he had an agenda. Robert and Gary, still on the surface watched him writing. Robert dropped down and Gary followed. The three of them formed a circle, then Jim flashed his slate that said, “What took you so long?” Robert and Gary smiled.

Gary quickly wrote, “Stopped for beer.”

Robert started laughing and noticed Jim was pushing himself for lack of air, but was holding out when he quickly scribbled, “You bastards.”

They were all laughing and then Jim kicked like crazy as he went for a breath of air. Robert liked the feel of the group and the humor was a good sign of being relaxed in the water and was very impressed with Jim’s stamina.

When they reached the surface, Nona was kneeling down on the side of the pool. Again, Robert thought of Beverly and Jim was probably thinking of getting Nona into trouble. She was smiling and said, “You guys are having too much fun down there. I was thinking about coming down.”

Gary said, “To save us?”

“Oh, no, I told you I wasn't going to get my hair wet, but felt I was missing a party.” She looked at Robert and raised her eyebrows.

It was hard to believe they had been in the water over two hours. They tightened their weight belts and started the swim toward the shallow end. Robert noted that even though they were tired from treading water they were still talking and laughing as they swam to the shallow end. Robert was thinking that it was time for Gary and Jim to order wetsuits for an ocean lesson. When they reached the shallow end they climbed the ladder, removed their weight belts, gently set them on lounge chairs, grabbed their towels and started drying off. Nona was standing near them.

Robert said, "Nona, thanks for letting us come in with our gear. It was very helpful."

"Oh, you're welcome. You coming back for more training?"

"Well, maybe, but I think these guys are ready for the ocean."

She said, "How long you been giving diving lessons?"

"What time is it now?"

She said, "About four."

"Well, we started at two, so I've been giving diving lessons for two hours."

Nona laughed and said, "I wouldn't mind trying that."

"I'm sure our team could use a fourth person. And you seem to have the vital qualification."

"What's that?"

Robert said, "A sense of humor."

Nona's smile suddenly turned to a serious look and said, "You know, that's a nice compliment. Nobody has ever told me that before. Thank you." Then she smiled and added, "But, you've never seen me early in the morning."

As they were driving away from the pool, Gary, in a high-pitched voice said, "But Robert, you haven't seen me early in the morning." Robert just smiled.

Jim said, "Yeah, I think it's that commando look. If they were going together, Robert would probably give her homemade writing slate and a grease pencil for her birthday so they could communicate." They laughed.

Jim continued, “But, I think you’re right Gary, she does like him, but you know who she goes with?”

Gary said, “No, who?”

Jim said, “Chuck Brandon, a Panther halfback.”

Robert remembered him from psychology class, but he didn’t know what a halfback was. He did know quarterback and center, but not what they called those other guys that run around the field. At least he did know that the Panthers were the Hartnell football team.

Robert said, “Well, I’m not afraid of those sissy football players and I’m particularly not afraid of Chucky.” They laughed. “You guys ready to order your wetsuits? We'll need them for the next training.”

For the first time today, Jim turned serious and said, “I’m still working on my parents about diving. You know, Robert, it might help if they met you"

Pacific Grove Dive Shop

After Jim’s parents met Robert, they apparently had confidence that Robert and Gary would take care of him, and gave Jim the money for his wetsuit and scuba equipment. Phillip and Ted, the owners of the dive shop, were in their early thirties and looked like divers should look. Prior to entering the shop, Jim and Gary were starting to think of themselves as divers, even though they had never been in the ocean. And they were doing an impressive job of acting the part. However, entering the dive shop on Lighthouse Avenue for the first time, and seeing the owners, put the two actors in their place. Robert was still very intimidated by them and never believed he would overcome the feeling. And it wasn't that the shop owners were obnoxious. They were really nice guys. But just as you could have cast Gary as a college student in a movie, these guys would have been cast as divers. And they not only had the look, with their thick black beards, they had the knowledge and pictures of them diving in Tahiti, Hawaii, Australia, Caribbean, and the Mediterranean. This was the first dive shop in Monterey and the two owners had foresight to see that Monterey Bay, even with its icy cold and often treacherous waters, was capable of supporting a dive shop. Not to mention that they believed this was the most beautiful diving water in the world and could eventually become a worldwide diver's dream. Fortunately for the young divers that hadn’t happened yet.

After getting into Gary’s red 1955 Plymouth four door, it didn't take long for the two of them to shake the intimidation of the dive shop owners and again became divers, even though it would be two to three weeks before their wetsuits would be ready, and then they had to get their scuba equipment. Being cautious, Robert recommended that they wait on spending money on scuba equipment until they have some ocean snorkeling experience.

Snorkeling the Cove

Early Saturday morning, Jim and Gary anxiously loaded their weight belts, masks, fins, and snorkels into Robert’s 1952 brown and white Chevy two-door hardtop. This was a monumental day, for their wetsuits were ready to be picked up at the dive shop. Fifteen minutes later, they were traveling down the Monterey Highway with Gary riding shotgun, Jim in the back seat and on their way for their first ocean snorkeling dive. Their wetsuits fit quite well and even if they hadn’t they probably would have taken them anyway, for they were very anxious for their first ocean experience. After leaving the dive shop, the two of them were able to shake the self-inflicted intimidation of the dive shop owners and become divers again, even then though they still haven’t been in the ocean.

Robert pulled his Chevy into the Cove parking lot. Each time he came to the Cove, he recalled the first time that he and his younger brother snorkeled here without wetsuits. The beauty of the scenery and the fifteen to twenty feet visibility seemed to overcome any sensation of the icy water. The exhilarating clear water, fish, starfish, sea urchins, and huge rocks enticed nearly thirty dives to the bottom that day. Robert’s continued appreciation of the ocean was further enhanced by his comparison of the ocean with Montana's Fort Peck Lake, where finding something to look at was a challenge. In Fort Peck Lake, Robert and his younger brother would get excited when they found a rusty beer can or a lost fishing lure, and on a good day, a school of minnows might swim by and on very good day, a pike.

The regulars, a group of older men and women were in place at the far end of the beach even though it was still an overcast day. Some of the men wore real skimpy swimsuits and they all had great tans even though Monterey never seemed to be a get-a-suntan paradise. The area where the regulars sit was somewhat sheltered from the wind and if Monterey decided to have sun that day, they would get it first. Although the regulars most likely just in lived in the neighborhood, Robert found it was more interesting to think of them as Guru or cult like with a spiritual side. He also figured they had a hand in keeping this beautiful spotless beach, immaculate.

The divers had swimsuits under their jeans and were standing near the rear of the Chevy anxiously waiting for Robert to open the trunk. Once the trunk was open they started pulling off their jeans and were struggling to pull on their new wetsuit trousers. Robert pulled out a plastic catsup squeeze bottle from his army surplus bag, aimed the bottle into each leg of his wetsuit, shot a puff of white powder like stuff inside.

Jim said, "Oh no. I can't believe it. Commando Guy using baby powder." Robert laughed and Gary looked inquisitive.

Robert said, "It's cornstarch, lubricates the inside of the wetsuit and makes it easier to get on." He handed the bottle to Gary, who used it, and passed it on to Jim. It didn't take Jim long to realize the squeeze bottle had the capability of being a deadly weapon and he got off two rounds to Gary's chest. The two became quite good at these cornstarch duels once they had their own bottles and a little practice. Each dual became more combative, unexpected and eventually a ritual before each dive.

Jim and Gary had purchased store-bought writing slates at the dive shop, but Robert stuck with his hand-crafted device because of his thriftiness and do-it-yourself upbringing, and it was doing the job. But he did have to admit he liked their new slates. They had their wetsuits on and then buckled on their weight belts. With their fins, snorkels, and masks in hand they started down the concrete steps to the beach below.

A pretty woman in her mid thirties, with two young kids, was sitting on a blanket in the middle of the beach. The kids had cute shovels and buckets and most likely all the divers noticed that the woman had appealing breasts. The divers walked around behind the family to the far end and picked a place to sit. The young kids were very interested in the trio and the new divers managed to look very diver like, and Jim gave them as much of a mature nod as he could muster up.

The smiling new divers wasted no time entering the beckoning water, but when the icy liquid reached their midsection and started seeping into their wetsuits, their smiles turned to grimace. As they spend more time in Monterey Bay they will have to make a choice between wading in or diving in. Robert preferred getting it over with quickly. Once the water completely saturates your wetsuit, within a few minutes your body will start warming the water to an almost tolerable temperature.

As they snorkeled toward the center of the cove, they were amazed at the visibility which was about fifteen feet. Robert said, “Okay, let’s meet near that large rock just below us. Looks like about ten feet down. When we get down there write a note to the group and then come back up. Don’t forget to clear your ears on the way down."

Once at the bottom, Robert wrote, “Ears okay?”

Both of them flashed the "Okay" hand signal by putting their thumb and index finger together.

Gary pointed and then wrote, "Fish.”

Jim wrote, “Forgot spear gun.” Actually, the divers knew that the Cove is part of a sanctuary in Monterey Bay so you weren't allowed to shoot fish or remove anything which almost made it like diving in an aquarium.

On the surface Robert said, "Now go back down to the same rock and fill your masks with water. Then clear them and return to the surface."

As their masks filled with water, Robert knew how they felt as the fifty-some degree water made contact with their faces. It is definitely a shock but a very good test of staying calm and relaxed in the water. Gary was able to get most of the water out, but Jim struggled a bit and finally surfaced with a mask half full. But in the Jim fashion, as soon as he hit the surface for a breath, he immediately dove again and came up with an empty mask.

Jim said, "It's a lot harder out here than the pool."

Robert said, "Okay, go down and do it again."

They flooded and quickly cleared their masks, but neither of them seemed to be in a hurry to surface, despite their need for air. Back on the surface, Robert reminded them to keep within sight of each other. Jim and Gary went down together and Robert followed. As they swam single file between two huge rocks that formed a small canyon, Jim spotted an unusual looking fish and started chasing it. They were down about fifteen feet and stayed down longer than normal because of incredible scenery and action of trailing the fish. As the new divers were checking crevices for sea life, Robert came along side Gary and pushed against his facemask to break the seal. His mask flooded with icy water, But Gary quickly resealed and cleared it. The Monterey Bay water temperature varies from the low fifties in winter to the high fifties in the summer. You just know it's, cold so a few degrees either way doesn't seem to make much difference. However, a diver should know that water temperature affects buoyancy slightly because as water gets colder it becomes denser and tends make a diver more buoyant. They spent about two hours in the water, which is quite a long time considering the water temperature, but the divers were captivated by the underwater landscape and sea life.

They swam toward shore, and as normal for the Cove, the waves were minimal so reaching the beach was quite easy. When the water was shallow enough Robert removed his fins and then let the gentle waves push him a little closer to the beach. Jim and Gary removed their fins and also drifted into shore. The divers sat at the edge of the water, removed their masks and then pulled off their hoods. Jim and Gary were worn out but grinning like crazy. Robert could see that the cold water had not diminished their enthusiasm. They removed their weight belts and then unzipped their wetsuit jackets and peeled off the wetsuit arms. The sun had come out and it felt good to get out of the jacket. Then they peeled their trousers down their legs and struggled as they pulled them over their feet. Robert's younger brother always said the good thing about diving is that it feels so good when it is over. And in some respects Robert agreed with him, but each time Robert finished a dive, he left the water feeling completely exhilarated.

Gary said, "That was great. I think it's time get the scuba gear."

Jim smiled and said, "Yep, better than sex."

Robert and Gary looked at each other and smiled that smile that doubted Jim had ever had sex. Robert didn't really know much about Jim's girlfriend, but he had double dated with Gary and his girlfriend and he doubted that Gary had ever had sex either. But he really didn't know, and these guys weren't the type to talk about it. Despite them having steady girlfriends, didn't make Robert anxious to get tied down. When he did go out with a girl, he wasn't looking for somebody to go steady with. He just wanted to go on a date. And if he had to choose between going on a date and diving, at this time in his life, he would choose diving. Well, maybe not.

After spending about an hour in the sun warming up, they picked up their diving gear and walked up the stairs to the parking lot. They retrieved their jeans and towels from the trunk, wrapped towels around themselves and slipped off their wet swimsuits and quickly stepped into their jeans. The salt residue covered their bodies and though some might not like that feeling, Robert liked it, for it made him feel more rugged than he really was. It was noon so they stopped at Hamburger Haven for hamburgers and French-fries. Diving always seemed to build up an appetite.

As they were driving back to Salinas Jim said, "What's next coach?"

Robert said, "It's time to get into some authentic Monterey water."

Snorkeling Point Pinos

Jim's1956 Oldsmobile, white, four-door hardtop with leather seats, a luxurious car with a powerful V-8, could have easily raced down the highway at ninety, but Jim held her at sixty five. Generally if a young person's first car is a four-door, it most likely was a hand me down from their parents when they bought a new car. Robert never had a hand me down because his dad never bought a new car. Jim parked on the side of the road near Point Pinos. The sun didn't look like it would come out, but at least the surf wasn't too bad, maybe breaking about two feet on the beach, but it was enough to give the divers a more realistic Monterey dive, as opposed to the peaceful, protected water at the Cove. Getting in and out of most Monterey Bay diving spots was often the most challenging part of a dive. Jim opened his trunk, and the new divers seemed to be in a real hurry as they stripped down to their swimsuits, and rightly so, because this time, they were armed with their brand new fully loaded squeeze bottles. Gary was Captain Catsup and Jim was Major Mustard. As Gary was slipping on his wetsuit trousers, two shots rang out from the mustard tip, hitting Gary in the legs. But now, Jim was vulnerable, for as he was slipping into his wetsuit trousers, Gary's catsup bottle showed no mercy as it gave Jim a blast to the stomach.

Jim said, "You bastard." Jim liked that word and it sounded good coming from him, even though none of the divers seemed to cuss very much. With his trousers pulled up, Jim crouched down for retaliation shot, but as he reached for his weapon, Gary squeezed off a final round, catching Jim right between the eyes.

Jim laughed and said, "I'll get you next time, varmint."

They carried their masks, fins and weight belts down to a small beach, watching the surf come in as they put on their equipment.

Robert said, "The bay gets quite rough and the waves breaking on the beach can easily knock you down. And if you have a scuba tank on your back and weights around your waist, it can be very difficult getting up."

The new divers had no problem as they carried their fins and waded through the waist high water, until it was deep enough to hurriedly put on their fins and swim out about a hundred feet to get beyond the surf that was intent on pushing them back to the beach. Once beyond the breakers, rolling waves moved the divers up and down but it seemed rather peaceful. However, the strong rip currents in the bay can carry a person out to sea, so that is another danger to keep in mind. The divers rolled with the waves, snorkeling and viewing the bottom and after numerous dives down to about fifteen feet and seeing some fairly large fish hiding in crevices, along with some incredible scenery, they were getting tired and it felt the seas had picked up quite a bit so they snorkeled toward the beach. They were able to catch a few waves and body surf until the water was shallow enough to stand, so they quickly removed their fins, and started walking and fighting against the outgoing water, but suddenly an incoming wave caught Jim and knocked him down. He managed to get up, but with a concerned look said, “Dropped a fin.”

Robert and Gary put their masks and fins back on and begin to search the shallow murky water that was stirred up by the breaking surf. They scanned the bottom for nearly ten minutes and luckily Gary spotted the fin that was covered with sand. He forced himself under, reached for it, stood up and proudly held up Jim’s fin as though he had a trophy fish.

Jim smiled and said, “Thanks buddy."

Gary said, “Looks like record a fin fish.”

Robert liked the way the grouped worked together to handle this situation and they did quite well in the surf even though it can get a whole lot rougher than it was today. And Jim was reminded to not turn his back on the sly surf. They got into Jim’s Olds and stopped at Hamburger Haven in Pacific Grove for hamburgers, fries, and cokes and a chance to chat with the girls who worked there. Jim let them know they had just come in from a dive, which seemed to impress the girls and they wanted to know if they saw any sharks. And living in Pacific Grove they knew about most the shark sightings from fishermen and beach goers that came in for burgers. So this always made the divers feel quite adventurous and it seemed to get them extra fries too.

Though both Gary and Jim had steady girlfriends, it was Jim's nature to flirt without any kind finesse. So Jim did most of the flirting, and Robert and Gary just were part of Jim's flirting support group, and they too benefited by meeting new people. But oddly enough, despite Jim's flirting, and humor and seemingly carefree attitude, once he got behind the wheel of his car, he became very serious, and the most cautious driver of the group.

Scuba Training Cove or Pool

Robert thought about having their first scuba dive in the Cove but decided the swimming pool would be much safer. Maybe his decision was based on something other than safety, for he knew the Cove would have been perfectly safe and a great place to start. Dismissing the idea that he may have ulterior motives, he pulled into the swimming pool parking lot knowing if somebody other than Nona was on duty, he would come back as often as necessary, but this must have been his lucky day, for as he opened the pool door, a sense of relief and warmth came over him as he walked toward her and said, “Hi, remember me?”

Nona said, “Hey it’s Commando Guy. I didn’t recognize you without your army gear.”

Robert laughed and said, “Oh, no. I didn’t know you overheard that stuff.”

Nona laughed and said, “I didn’t miss a thing that day.” A smiled remained on her face and she continued, “So are your friends real divers now?”

Robert nodded, smiled and said, “They're doing pretty good. We've been doing some ocean snorkeling.”

“Where do you do that?”

“Well, we trained in the Cove at Pacific Grove to start with.”

“Yeah, I know where that is, but it has been a long since I’ve been over there. I mean over to Monterey or Pacific Grove.”

“That’s too bad. Maybe we could go there sometime and get a hamburger and take a walk on the beach.”

She smiled and said, “That sounds like fun, but I don’t know if Chuck, you know, my boyfriend, would like that."

"Oh, yeah, that's probably not a good idea."

Nona said, "All I do is work, go to school and attend football games. Maybe I have my priorities wrong.”

“Well, at least you're on the right track. I mean doing the right things with school an all."

"Yeah, I guess, but it seems like I don't have any control of my life."

"Well, it won't always be like that."

She smiled, but now had a longing look her eyes and a little moisture but then changed the subject and said, “So did you just come out to visit so you could make me jealous of you and your friends’ great adventures?”

Robert thought to himself that good old humor helps out again. Sometimes it’s a great way to keep from crying. Robert smiled and said, “That’s right and it seems to be working. But really, I wondered if we could use your pool again for Jim and Gary’s first scuba dive.”

"Oh, another unusual request, is there nothing normal about you?”

Robert hesitated and put on his best perplexed look, and after a couple of seconds said, “You know, can’t think of a thing.”

Nona laughed, and said, “Well, let’s ask my boss, Mr. Kirsten. He's right over there.”

Mr. Kirsten looked to be in his early forties and seemed much nicer than Chester, and he didn’t appear to have the lust for Nona, that a jerk like Chester would have had. It sort of gave Robert a little more confidence and respect for city employees. Robert explained they would like to spend about two hours in the pool to get acquainted with their scuba gear.

Mr. Kirsten said, "And you're their instructor?"

Robert said, “Yes sir.”

“How long have you been diving?”

Robert was relieved that he didn't ask how long he had been an instructor and said, “I started using scuba gear when I was twelve.”

Mr. Kirsten said, “That’s a long time. I have to admit that I don’t know anything about scuba diving, but I guess there isn’t much that could wrong in a swimming pool.”

Robert didn’t want to expand Mr. Kirsten’s knowledge or complicate the issue, so he didn’t mention that it was possible for a person using scuba equipment in a swimming pool to get an air embolism, which could damage their lungs if they forget to exhale air during an ascent. And this could easily happen if panic sets in and they rush to the surface.

Robert said, “That’s why I'd rather they did their first scuba dive in a safe place like your pool rather starting out in the ocean.”

“Sounds okay to me, but I'd like to be here when you do it. I’m interested in seeing it. I think we should schedule it before the pool opens if Nona is willing to put in some extra time.” He raised his eyebrows as he looked at Nona.

She smiled and said, “Oh sure Mr. Kirsten.”

“Nona knows my schedule, so work out a time with her that she can come in a couple hours before the pool opens. And Robert, would it be okay if I brought my boys to see it? They would really enjoy that. Maybe my wife would too.”

Robert smiled and said, “Oh, sure, that’s fine with me. Thank you Mr. Kirsten.”

Scuba Training

Though they had their tanks charged the last time they were in Monterey, Robert had them attach his pressure gauge to each tank to ensure they still had a full charge. Then they shut the scuba tank valve, bled off the pressure and removed the pressure gauge. They ensured the o-ring was in place and attached their regulators. Jim and Gary had new single hose regulators, but when Robert pulled his regulator from his dive bag, he could see Jim's mind working for some commando humor, for Robert had a seven-year old, Dive Air dual hose regulator.

Jim, trying to hold on to a straight face said, "This is starting to look like the first season of Sea Hunt."

Gary said, "Yeah, it looks like Lloyd Bridges. I mean Mike Nelson."

The diver's comments were cut short by Mr. Kirsten coming in with his wife and two sons. The divers tried not to stare at Mrs. Kirsten, for she was very attractive, but as you might expect, Jim didn't do such a good job of hiding his observation.

Mr. Kirsten said, "This is my wife, Kate and our two sons, Peter and Dennis."

Peter was trying to whisper to his little brother, but everybody could hear him, when he said, "Wow, look Dennis. Look at those two hoses. He must be a frogman. You know, like in the war movies. And look, an Army belt."

Even though they didn't have the buoyancy of wetsuits to overcome, Robert still had them wear their weight belts, for he wanted them to have plenty of negative buoyancy so they wouldn't accidentally bob to the surface. They helped each other put the tanks on and tighten the straps. And then they put on their weight belts, and Robert explained to the audience that the weight belt goes on after the tank so that it can be quickly released in an emergency.

Mrs. Kirsten seemed very interested in the diving equipment. She moved close to Gary, put her hand on his tank, and as he inhaled her delicate scent, she said, “This is fascinating, but I don’t think that I could go down and breathe with that big thing in my mouth.” Her words were wasted on Gary, as he felt her arm brush against him and the warmth of her body as she moved her hand to his back and said, “You guys be careful.”

Robert held his mask in place, jumped into the deep end of the pool and moved out of the way as he waited for Jim and Gary. Once they were all in the water, Robert said, "Go down and stand on the bottom for a while to get used to breathing. And make sure you exhale on the way up."

As soon as they stopped treading water, they quickly dropped feet first because they were so heavy. Robert could see they were squeezing their noses to clear their ears as they dropped down. Of course going to ten feet doesn’t take very long, and soon the spectators could see the divers standing on the bottom. Robert gave the okay signal with his thumb and index finger to ensure they were doing okay. They responded with okay. They each had their writing slates hanging on their side.

Robert wrote, “Keep tank off bottom.”

The divers signaled okay. Robert watched their eyes and they both seemed relaxed.

Jim wrote, “Great.”

Gary wrote, “Yeah.”

Robert wrote, "Go up slow and exhale.”

When they broached Robert said, “Remember to not come up any faster than your bubbles." They submerged again and slowly moved along the pool bottom. Jim waved at the visitors a few times, and the young boys looking down from the surface, chuckled and waved back, and then Mrs. Kirsten waved. Jim and Gary swam together with Robert following. The boys were walking around the pool ledge watching the divers and tracking their air bubbles. They had been down about twenty minutes when they heard a loud splash, and saw a swimmer coming toward them. It was Nona. She swam around to Jim and Gary, touched them, and then approached Robert and put her face up against his mask. He took off his mask and put his face close to hers for a few seconds before she ran out air and shot to the surface. Robert went to each diver and pulled their facemasks away, but neither panicked when the water rushed in, and they immediately cleared their masks. The divers were enjoying their new adventure of breathing underwater so much their air seemed to run low before they realized and were forced to surface. It is important to leave a few hundred pounds of air inside the tank to limit moisture and it's also important to not run out of air while you are down.

Mrs. Kirsten again stood next to Gary, and as she was thanking the group, placed her hand on his shoulder and said, "Oh, you're so cold. You should go in and take a hot shower." She looked into Gary's eyes, smiled and raised her eyelids.

Nona, a smile on her face, had a towel around her shoulders, her hair was still dripping water, and she was still looking great.

After Mr. Kirsten and his family left, Robert was standing near Nona and said, "Thanks for your visit down there. Sure improved the pool scenery."

She smiled and said, "That was fun. I'm glad you guys came by. If you need any more training, let me know." She moved close to Robert, grabbed his writing slate and wrote down her home number.

As the divers pulled away from the pool parking, Gary said, "Robert, I remember you saying you drink beer. Is that right?"

"Sure"

"Well, Jim and I managed to get a twelve pack of Coors that we've had on ice for a while. Sort of a celebration and a thank you for your instruction."

Robert said, "That's a relief. For a while there, I was starting to worry that you guys weren't drinkers."

Jim said, "Well, I think you'll find we are better drinkers than divers." They laughed.

Beer at Gary's

A Sam Cooke song, "That's the sound of the men working on the chain gang," is playing when Robert knocks on the door.

He hears Gary yell, "Come on in."

Jim said, "Hey it's Commando Guy."

Robert smiles and notices that they hadn't started drinking yet, or at least there was no evidence that he could see. Gary went to a cooler that was sitting at the end of the couch, proudly opened the lid and they all looked at the beautiful sight of iced beer. It seems like beer on ice always tastes colder and better than out of a refrigerator. Gary picked up a beer, expertly opened it with a church key that was attached to his keychain, handed it to Robert, opened a second for Jim's outreached hand, and finally one for himself before closing the lid. They sat around a coffee table with Jim and Gary on a leather couch and Robert in a stuffed chair across from them.

Gary held up his beer and said, "Here's thanks to Robert for his diving instruction and introducing us to what I'll remember as a great part of my life."

Jim said, "That's goes for me too." They tipped their beers, took a healthy sip, and were quiet as they took a second sip.

Robert, somewhat emotionally said, "Thanks for the beer and thanks for becoming my diving buddies. Except for my younger brother when we were in grade school doing some serious pool and lake diving, I've never really had a diving buddy, let alone two diving buddies. And thanks to Gary, I think I've found the best guys for the job."

Jim and Gary, very seriously and simultaneously said, "Thanks, Robert."

Gary said, "Did you actually make that weight belt yourself?"

"Yeah, my younger brother and I have made several."

Gary said, “You made the weights too?”

“Yeah, we had over twenty feet of lead water pipe that we picked up when they replaced our water pipes in Montana. We made a mold out of wood, melted the lead and poured the lead into the mold.”

Jim said, “How'd you melt the lead?”

Robert said, "We used an old coffee can with vice grips for a handle and then heated the lead with my dad’s acetylene torch.”

Jim said, "That's pretty ingenious, Commando Guy."

"Well, we were lucky. Our dad being a mechanic, machinist, and welder we learned a lot from him and he let use whatever tools he had in his shop."

Jim shook his head and said, “Breathing underwater. This was a great day, and I can’t wait to get to the ocean.”

Robert, said, “Well, that’s the next stop.”

Gary said in a very serious tone, “You know, Jim and I were talking before you came in and thought we could have done our first scuba dive in the Cove since that place is like a swimming pool.”

Robert said, “Yeah, I thought about that.”

Gary, still serious, continued, “Well, our theory is that you have a thing for Nona. And today was an excuse to go back there.”

“Yeah, I thought about that. But really I wanted to make sure that we started out right. Even Lloyd Bridges did his first scuba dive in a pool, and Cousteau too."

Jim and Gary laughed, not exactly because of what he said, but because he was so serious about it.

Robert continued, “But speaking of a girl or I should say a woman, and not an ordinary woman, but a very attractive woman, Gary, you seemed to have plenty going on with Mrs. Kirsten.”

“Gary said, “What are you talking about?”

Jim said, “Come on Gary, I thought that woman was gonna crawl into your swimsuit.”

Gary said, “Well she had to stand somewhere and she was interested in my equipment.”

Jim with a smirk-like smile raised his eyebrows, and said "Your equipment?"

Gary said, "I'm talking about my diving equipment."

Jim nodded with disbelief, "Oh, oh yeah, okay."

Gary continued, "And she probably felt safer with me than she would have next to Commando Guy or you, Jim.”

Jim said, “Well she sure was hanging on you.”

Gary said, “Well, everybody has a different comfort zone. But between her comfort zone and those very tight jeans and the blouse that was opened about one button too many, yeah, Kate Kirsten had my attention.” Gary took the final gulp of his beer and said, “Hey, how about another beer?"

Jim said, “Robert, would you get the accused another beer, and get one for me too. And get one for yourself. Hell, get all of us another beer.”

Gary said, “What I really think is that she was merely using me. Kate was intrigued by those big hoses on Robert’s regulator.”

Robert said, "No, no. The kids were.”

Gary said, "It's no mystery that our skimpy little hoses on our modern regulators are no match for your big hoses. Those hoses are unnatural, scary, yet intriguing. She couldn’t resist staring those monsters, but felt the need to admire them from a safe distance. And it wasn't only those hoses she was afraid of. No, it was Commando Guy. She could see it in his steely eyes that he could snap at any time and reach for that homemade knife, that is encased in that Army surplus scabbard that hangs from that Army surplus belt"

Gary stood up and took off his glasses and shook his head. Then he put his glasses back on. "Just imagine the torture that poor Kate was going through. Wishing she was standing next to Commando Guy so she could reach for a masculine ribbed hose with her small soft hand that was amply coated with Jergin's Lotion. That poor woman strolled into that swimming pool like an angel and was transformed into a hungry animal. But, I don't deny that I was lusting after Kate as her hand touched my shoulder. And when she asked about my equipment, no I wasn't thinking scuba."

Jim said, "Robert that was very clever using Kate as a diversion to skirt the original question, which was, why we went to the pool rather than the Cove for our first scuba dive."

Gary said, "Did it have something to do with a girl named Nona? What would have caused a beautiful, intelligent, rational girl, whose main long-term goal as a lifeguard, is to not get her hair wet, suddenly take a plunge into the deep, treacherous water of the pool and perform an obligatory wave to Jim and I, and then, despite desperateness for a breath of air, continue even further down to visit Commando Guy, who was lurking on the bottom like a hungry moray eel?"

Robert said, "Well, Nona may have had something to do with it. But she's way out of my league."

Gary said, "Something to do with it? Think about it. Monterey Bay is in the Red Triangle where great white sharks hang out."

The Red Triangle, named for the blood in the water after a shark attack, is a triangular shaped 120 mile stretch along the California coast where an estimated eleven percent of all recorded great white shark attacks in the entire world and thirty eight percent in the United States, have occurred. And several attacks by great whites have occurred in the Monterey area.

Gary continued, "My point is, part of the reason Robert dives, is the risk of great white sharks. Now the question is, would he go out with

Nona, because of the risk involved? Perhaps to Robert, Chucky is the great white shark."

Robert said, "Jim, we've got to get him out of that psychology class. Is it time for another beer?"

Jim said, "I'll drink to that." Gary fetched three more beers.

Robert said, "Gary, Mrs. Kirsten was hitting on you. And, you might think about getting a new swimsuit."

Jim said, "Yeah, I noticed that too."

Gary said, "What do mean? What's wrong with my swimsuit?"

Jim said, "Well, they're quite short. And it wouldn't take much persuasion for something to stick its nose out the bottom of those skimpy trunks for a look around."

Gary concerned, said, "No, it couldn't have."

Jim said, "Oh, really?"

Gary said, "Come on, this isn't funny. It couldn't have."

Jim said, "Yeah, you're probably right. Just funny that both of us thought we saw something. But, it was probably nothing."

Beach Walk with Nona

Robert had volunteered to take the tanks to Monterey and drop them off at the dive shop for the next dive. About noon on Sunday, he picked up the phone and the voice said, "Hi, this is Nona."

Robert replied in a very surprised tone, "Nona?"

"Yeah, you know, the pool girl."

"Yeah, but I didn't expect you to call."

"I know. I shouldn't have. Girls aren't supposed to call guys."

Robert stuttered a bit and said, "No, I'm glad you did. I'm just so surprised."

"Robert, I don't want you to get the wrong idea, but I was wondering if we could, or if you are interested in doing that Monterey beach walk you talked about? Chuck went to visit his parents, and I thought it would be enjoyable. I know it's short notice and you probably already have plans so we could do it some other time."

He said, "Oh, no, that sounds good. I get so wrapped up in the diving that I sort of forget about planning other things. Maybe we could go over early and then get something to eat after we take a walk."

"Are you sure?"

"Yeah, definitely. I'd like to see you." I could pick you up about two if that's okay."

"I'll be ready."

He pulled alongside the curb in front of Nona's house and took a few deep breaths. Then he got out, went to the door and knocked. He did see the door bell button on the side wall, but he wasn't fond of door bells because if you can't hear it from outside you don't know if it works, but you hesitate to push it again. Seemed to him that knocking again is okay, but ringing again is risky. All those deep thoughts were not necessary, for within seconds Nona came to the door, took his hand and guided him inside and without any hesitation said, "Mom, Dad, this is my friend Robert." This was awkward to Robert considering she was going with Chuck, but her parents seemed very receptive and nice. He seemed to be the only one worrying about it.

Nona said, "Robert, I'll be right back. I have to get my sweater."

Nona's Dad said, "Nona said you're a scuba diver instructor from Montana."

Robert was caught off guard, wondering how she knew he was from Montana, but finally said, “Well, I do have a couple of students. But I haven't been doing it very long. I mean I've been diving a long time but being an instructor is something new.”

Nona’s Dad smiled with distant expression, “And Montana, huh. What part?”

Robert said, “Northeastern, a town called, Glasgow.”

Nona’s Dad nodded thoughtfully and said, “That’s some cold and windy country. I grew up in North Dakota. Still have a brother and some relatives there.” Her Dad continued, "I ended up in the Navy on submarines when I got out of high school. Your scuba diving reminded me of the UDT guys we carried. You know the Underwater Demolition Teams. I always admired those guys. I mean the places they had to go and things they did."

Robert replied, “UDTs, yes sir that’s an elite group. But, submarine service, well, that’s an elite group too. I’ve never known anybody that was on submarines. You have to volunteer for that, don’t you?”

He said, “Yeah, all volunteers and that’s probably why they have a pretty good group of guys. I liked the small crew and they usually had good food. But after drinking powered milk and eating powdered eggs for a month or so, it makes you appreciate the fresh stuff a little more. We did some interesting things. It was a good part of my life"

Nona returns and said, "I'm finally ready."

Nona's Dad held out his hand and said, "It was nice meeting you Robert."

Nona's Mom smiled, shook Robert's hand and said, "You two have a nice time."

As they drove through town toward the Monterey Highway, Robert said, “Your dad and mom seem nice."

"Yeah, I think they are."

"It is sort of strange though. You going with Chuck and then I show up."

"Well, I don't think they are real fond of Chuck, but they don't say much about it. They let me make my own decisions, but this is the first time that I have brought another guy to the house so I didn't really know what they would think."

"So, I was a test case?"

"Yes, that's right. I wanted to see the expression on their faces. I'm doing a paper for my psychology class. Next week I'm bringing over the guy that has the Chevy with the big tires on the rear and the flames painted on the doors and the engine makes a lot of noise." Robert laughed and Nona continued, "No, I knew they would like you. I told them you were my friend. And that's true, I think." She raised her eyebrows in a questioning manner and he smiled and nodded. She continued, "I do know that Chuck doesn't know that my dad was on submarines, nor does Chuck care that he was on submarines."

Robert nodded, and said, "Well, I've never known anybody that did that. I think that's pretty neat."

"Well, he doesn't talk about it much, but he seemed to like talking with you." Robert was still curious about how she knew he was from Montana, but he didn't want to bring it up for it didn't really matter anyway. It certainly wasn't a big secret.

"I'm gonna stop off at the dive shop to drop off our tanks for refill."

She said, "Oh, that'll be interesting."

"You must remember Monterey weather because I see you brought a sweater."

She said, "Yeah, I don't like to be cold. But I think the fog and cold are part of the Monterey charm and it helps keep the tourists away."

He nodded and said, "Yeah, I never thought about that. That's probably true, especially the beach people." Robert pulled into a parking spot near the dive shop. They got out of the car and Robert opened the trunk and the three scuba tanks were side by side with the valves facing the rear of the car. He said, “We put the valves facing toward the rear in case you have to hit the brakes hard which could cause the tanks to shift forward and break the valves off.”

She nodded and said, “Oh, yeah. That makes sense.”

He pulled out one of the tanks, handed it to Nona and picked up the other two and they headed toward the shop.

She said, "These are heavy."

"Yeah, and once they are filled they are even heavier."

Nona, "Why, it's just air?"

"Well even air has weight. And as you fill the tank, the air compresses and gets noticeably heavier."

"Oh, yeah, never thought about that."

"You really notice the difference when you're in the water because you start getting more buoyant as you use air."

As they walked into the dive shop, Phillip was behind a counter, looked up and said, “So, you traded up for a new diving buddy, huh?”

Robert laughed and said, “Yeah, those two were starting to wear on me. This is Nona."

Phillip laughed and said, “I’m Phillip, nice to meet you Nona. You dive too?”

“Oh, no, I’m just here for the ride and to carry the tanks.”

Phillip smiled and said, "Well, there are a couple of women divers that come in. They're from San Francisco, and we would actually like to see more. Maybe you could get your boyfriend there to talk you into diving.” Nona smiled at Phillip and then raised her eyebrows at Robert.

After leaving the dive shop, they headed for Asilomar beach and parked the car on the side of the road, without getting too far into the sand, because it's easy to get stuck. As they started walking down the beach, they put on their sweaters, since the chilly fog was starting to roll in, and it almost seemed stormy.

Nona said, "Robert, I mean boyfriend." He laughed. Nona continued, "You know, that day at the pool when you were standing next to Jim and Gary, you stood out because you have that independent look. You're an innovator. I mean it's easy to be a consumer of trends and things and become one of the sheep. You started me thinking about my life. I'm a consumer. I'm one of the sheep. I don't even make my own plans as to what I'm going to do. Other people like Chuck are doing that for me. And Chuck, well he's following someone else, too. I don't know. You just got me thinking." They stopped and faced each other.

He said, "Don't you think I'd rather be a star football player?"

She laughed and said, "Oh, no. You're comfortable with yourself. And that's what makes you special. You don't have to act because you know how to be yourself. There's some kind of honesty about you that's hard to explain. It's just something I feel. And I like what I feel because you make me think. You bring out my more adventurous side, my wild side."

Robert said, "Your wild side?"

She put on her best pouting face with the lower lip sticking out, and said, "Yeah, my wild side. You think I don't have a wild side?

Robert smiled and said, "You're starting to scare me."

She laughed and said, "Well, maybe you should be scared."

He said, "Nona, I think what you are describing is a loner. And being a loner can be very depressing. I spend a lot of Saturday nights by myself. I guess by choice, but not always. I guess I tend to wonder what's around the corner. If I weren't that way, I might not be walking with you right now."

Nona nodded and said, "That's true. You would have made plans ahead of time."

Robert continued, "What seems odd is that there does not seem to be any middle choice. So it's either lonely or suffocated." Then he wished he hadn't used the word suffocated.

She stopped walking, faced him, tipped her head a little and their lips touched gently for a few seconds, then they hugged. As they held each other she whispered in his ear, "I don't want to suffocate you, but some part of me has to taste something different. I need some encouragement that I will eventually take control of my life."

They sat down, he put his arm around her, and she snuggled against his shoulder. They sighed and shared warmth of each other as the powerful ocean beat against the beach and rocks. A feeling of content and completeness came over him with the ocean in view, and somebody he enjoyed being with next to him. The feeling was somewhat frightening because now a three-piece puzzle made up the image that previously only required two pieces. What happens then one piece of the puzzle is missing? Maybe this was the middle choice or maybe Gary was right about swimming with the sharks. Then he forced the spinning thoughts from his mind, relaxed and allowed himself to enjoy being with her.

He said, "You ever read any Ayn Rand books?"

Nona said, "Yeah, she wrote, 'Atlas Shrugged' and 'Fountain Head'. I did read Fountain Head. She's such an interesting and independent person. Came from Russia, right?"

He said, "Yeah, she did."

She looked a little puzzled and said, "What brought her up?"

"Well, being with you reminds me of something. I was on a bus coming from Santa Barbara about a year ago. I went there to visit some college dropout friends that were wandering around the country. Coming home, I sat next to this college student. He was about my age and from South Africa. We talked about Ayn Rand's books and capitalism, and similar things for at least two hours. It was the most meaningful conversation I'd ever had. I guess I get the impression I could talk to you about anything. It's hard to find people that I enjoy talking with."

Nona nodded and said, “Thanks. I know what you mean about finding someone to talk with. I don’t really have anyone that seems to have the same interests that I have. I found out early on that Chuck is not a conservative and I can’t remember what I said, but it definitely riled him. And that might be one of the reasons we never had real conversations for fear of offending each other. I think he was indoctrinated by his overbearing father. I’m glad to know that we are playing on the same team. It seems the more I’m around you, the more I’ll want to be around you.”

He said, “I’m surprised. I’m glad, but surprised.”

She said, “I’m afraid if I’m around you too much I might turn into more than your friend. So, I think you're right. There doesn’t seem to be any middle ground. But since I can't be your friend there's only one other thing that we can do."

His eyes seemed to sadden a bit and he said, "Yeah, you're right. I understand. It's best if we stay away from each other."

She shook her head and said, “No, that won’t work. You’re not going to get rid of me that easy Commando Guy. Why can't we be lovers or something in between? How about, frovers?

Robert said, "Now you're really scaring me."

Nona laughed and said, "See, I do have a wild side. You bring it out in me. We don't have to decide anything right now. Maybe take a beach walk now and then for therapy. Play the cards as they’re dealt." She raised her eyebrows questioningly, "I need more in my life than the frivolous fluff I now have. I need to be around someone I enjoy being with. I need someone that can handle talking politics without getting pissed off."

He smiles, nods and repeated, “Pissed off and frivolous fluff.”

She smiled, “Yeah, frivolous fluff. You got a problem with that?”

He shook his head and said, “No, sir. I sure don’t.”

She kissed him and said, "I don’t want to confuse you, but I want to be with you once in a while. Can we do that?”

He said, “Don’t worry about confusing me. I’m a master at confusing myself. Nona, I'll be available. But I don't want to mess up your life. I won't call you and bother you."

Nona kissed him and said, “You can me anytime. Okay?"

Scuba Diving the Cove

Robert pulled the Chevy into the dive shop parking lot so they could pick up the tanks. The Dive Shop novelty had not worn off, for the three of them walked around and checked out the pictures, most of which they already seen, and then looked to see if they had any new equipment that the owners might have gotten in. The shop was beginning to look like a complete store compared to the sparse furnishings when they first opened.

Phillip said, “I see you went back to your old diving buddies.” Jim and Gary, with a confused look, glanced over at Robert. He continued, “Where you guys going today?”

Robert said, “The Cove for a little more training and some sightseeing.”

Phillip said, “I never get tired of going in there. It’s a very peaceful place with great scenery.” As they were carrying the tanks out, Phillip said, “You guys have a good time. You going to drop off the tanks afterwards?”

Gary said, “Yeah, if you're gonna be open?”

"Oh, yeah, we’ll be open until five.”

They loaded the tanks into the trunk and started for the Cove. Gary said, “What was he talking about in there? About going back to your diving buddies?”

Robert said, “Well, Nona called me the other day and wanted to go for ride to Monterey. She helped me carry the tanks into the dive shop”

Gary continued, “Were you gonna tell your diving buddies about this?”

Robert said, “No, I wasn’t. In fact, I forgot about it.”

Gary said, “Oh, yeah, I can see how that might happen."

Jim said, “Yeah, sure, that's something that could easily slip your mind." Robert smiled.

The Cove was quiet with the traditional locals gradually arriving at one end near the sea wall to worship the morning sun or perhaps pray for some morning sun. And it almost looked like the fog might lift enough for it to peak through. Robert opened the Chevy’s trunk and the three divers started stripping down to their swimsuits, all hoping they remembered to put on their swimsuits before leaving home. Forgetting to put on swimsuits wasn’t dive canceling serious, but inconvenient because you had to wrap a towel around yourself and do some awkward moving around to get into your wetsuit trousers.

Jim was the first to notice that Gary had a new swimsuit and said, “Nice swimsuit, Gary.”

Gary didn’t even smile so Jim left it at that, thinking he might harass him about it later. They attached the regulators to the tanks turned on the air to test o-ring seal took a couple of breaths to make sure the regulators were operating properly, and then put on their wetsuit jackets. With one arm through one of the tank straps, they swung the scuba tanks around on their backs and then put their other arm through the other strap. And finally they attached their weight belts and carried their mask and fins as they walked down the long set of stairs to the Cove beach. Gary was also carrying an inner tube that he thought would be handy to have.

Though not looking forward to the shock of the cold water, the anticipation of their first ocean scuba dive seemed to ease their reluctance, and without hesitation, they took the plunge, put on their facemasks, and paddled out on their backs. Once the water became deep enough they stopped, slipped on their fins, and continued out where the water was about twenty feet deep. The three of them gathered around the inner tube with their masks raised.

Robert said, "I guess this is it. Let's meet at the bottom and check your buoyancy. If you're too light find a rock and stick it inside your suit. Make sure you go down slow enough to keep your ears cleared." Robert put his facemask in place and checked the seal of the mask against his face by breathing in through his nose. Then he let himself sink feet first until he was under a few feet and then went into a pike position and started using his fins to propel toward the bottom. He found a large rock to sit on and watched the two divers above him flounder a bit on the surface. Jim started down first and Robert watched him squeeze his nose to clear his ears and kick toward him and settled into a standing position near Robert. Gary seemed to be fighting a little on the way down, indicating that he was light. Robert spotted a rock that didn't have many barnacles attached, picked it up and handed it to Gary when he was close enough. Gary nodded, took the rock, unzipped his wetsuit jacket and took on an agonizing expression as the cold water seeped through the open zipper. He quickly slipped the rock inside his jacket and zipped it back up. As they stood facing each other, Robert signaled okay with his fingers and they both responded with okay.

Jim reached for his slate and wrote, "Nice swimsuit." Gary was forced into a smile, Robert laughed, and was pleased to see they were relaxed as they experienced their first scuba dive in the ocean.

Gary, anxious to get past the swimsuit subject, reached for his slate and wrote, "Nona?" Robert started laughing and shook his head. He could see that these two guys were very relaxed in the water as they breathed through their mouths, which some might find unnatural, and their humor was intact.

Robert wrote, "Talked."

Jim wrote, "What about?"

Robert wrote, "You two weirdoes."

The new divers discovered the difficulties of laughing underwater with a mouthpiece in your mouth. The more relaxed you are in the water, the better you will be at handling an emergency. Being relaxed also reduces the amount of air usage, and panic breathing will drain your tank very quickly. With the small talk out of the way, the divers started making the most of their valuable air time. Jim and Gary had been previously exposed to the Cove, but now with the tanks strapped to their backs, they were able to stay down and become more than a brief part of the underwater environment. Robert stayed behind the two of them as they made their way to deeper water, and went their separate ways to take in the vast and beautiful scenery. Yet, he watched them continue to make sure they were always in sight of each other. Gary got Jim's attention as he was hovering over a small cave like hole in the side of a huge rock. He motioned Jim over and then looked over at Robert and motioned him. They both swam toward Gary who had found a moray eel whose head bobbed in and out of his den, searching for passing food. Gary had discovered the secret of slow observation and had the patience for a slow steady pace. Jim was a little hastier in his search to see a little bit of everything. The eel was quite a find and something that you wouldn't see on every dive. The entire Cove was much like an endless aquarium with its sea life and background of kelp and rocks. The beauty and peacefulness of the Cove was spectacular. Unlike other dive areas they would be going to, they didn't have to concern themselves with an unruly ocean that within thirty to forty minutes could go from small waves to very large, and often scary waves. The large rocks in the Cove form caverns that you can swim through and these caverns are often homes for larger fish.

Though, it didn't seem they had been out very long, the clear water, beautiful scenery, and the ability to breathe underwater, made the time go fast and Jim signaled that his air was running low. Robert signaled them to come over and once they stood together, he signaled to go up and the divers slowly and calmly started for the surface. Jim and Gary were both grinning as they hit the surface and flipped their masks up to locate the inner tube. As they hung on the tube, their grins turned to chatter of describing the beauty and adventure of being part of the underwater environment.

After dropping off their tanks for refill, they were on the Monterey Highway heading for Salinas. Robert was quiet and thankful that the Nona topic was on hold, as Jim and Gary competed for talk time in describing the dive. As beautiful as the Cove was, it was much like the bunny hill on a ski mountain, when compared to the other diving locations in Monterey Bay. As the two of them chattered about the dive, Robert was having pleasant thoughts of Nona.

Meeting Alexia

The divers had finished diving near the Coast Guard Pier, which is off Cannery Row, and were removing their wetsuits, when they noticed a pickup truck parked next to an old cannery that wasn't there when they started the dive. And then they saw a woman carrying a large box up the side stairway of the cannery. Normally changing from their wetsuits and swimsuits to their dry underwear and jeans was not a problem in this area because there was seldom anyone around. If they ever did see anyone it would be a homeless person that had taken refuge in one of the deserted canneries for the night. They managed to make the switch from wetsuits to jeans during one of her trips inside the cannery. They watched her return to her truck that was still quite full of large boxes and there was even a large stuffed chair near cab of the truck.

Jim yelled, “Need some help?”

Alexia smiled, and yelled back, “You know, I really could."

The three of them put on their shoes, slipped their tee shirts over their heads, and walked across to where her truck was parked.

The woman smiled and said, "These boxes of books are quite heavy and I didn’t know how I was going to get the chair up there. But you guys must have better things to do than help a desperate woman”

Gary said, “Not that we know of. We finished doing what we like to do best and anything else can wait.”

“Oh, thank you. I'm Alexandria, but most just call me Alexia. You guys live in Monterey?”

Gary said, “No, Salinas but come over here nearly every weekend to dive.”

She said, "So we have Jim, Gary, and Robert. It’s nice to meet all of you. You are the first signs of life, except for the sea gulls and sea lions that I’ve seen today."

They each picked up a box and followed Alexia up the stairway that led to a large landing and a door. Robert was directly behind her as she walked up the stairs. Though he was carrying a large box that partially blocked his view, he was able to notice that she looked as good from the rear as she did from the front.

“You guys are like angels. I had no idea how I would get this stuff into the loft." She had previously propped the door open with a rubber doorstop. Once they were all inside the loft, which was a very large open area, they set the boxes down, Alexia said, “This room was my grandfather’s office. As you can see there is a kitchen and then there are two baths back in that corner. But other than that, it’s this huge open space. I visited him quite often during the summer when I was young because I loved being near the ocean. He loved Monterey and the cannery industry and when he had to close his cannery, it was downhill for him. My family lives in Ohio. My grandfather always asked my Dad to move out here, but my Dad was established. I guess I was more interested in the cannery and this area than any of his other grandchildren. So when grandfather died, he gave me the cannery. I was shocked and had no idea what I would do with a cannery in Monterey when I lived in Ohio. But sometimes destiny takes over and here I am.”

The three of them looked as though they felt sorry for her and she picked up on that and said, “What you have to understand is that I love Monterey.” When Alexia mentioned destiny, Robert started thinking of all the pieces that had to fall into place for him to end up diving in Monterey Bay. The divers made several more trips up and down the stairs until they had emptied the truck. Alexia said, “I don’t know how to thank you. I don’t have any cokes or anything.”

Gary said, “Don’t worry about it. Didn’t hurt us a bit and it was nice meeting you.” Jim and Robert nodded their heads in agreement.

“Well, thank you all so much.”

As Gary guided his Plymouth down the Monterey Highway toward Salinas, Jim said, “Now that’s a real woman," Robert and Gary both nodded in agreement.

Gary and Jim were saying something about the dive, but Robert had tuned them out as he was still thinking about Alexia's destiny as compared to his own. He imagined the events that had to take place to get each of them to Monterey. It was as though they had something in common with each other. And to top off the coincidence, they end up meeting each other. He wondered if certain things that happen and people you meet are just random or are they meant to be? Of course she would never know of their coincidence.

Scuba Diving Point Pinos

Point Pinos was one of the diving spots that could be very peaceful upon submerging and forty minutes later you could surface to very extreme waves. And sometimes fog moved in so thick in a short time that you could no longer see land. And when the fog came in, it seemed that the water was often so calm that it is difficult to tell which direction was toward shore. So if you started swimming the wrong direction, you could be in trouble. This is when the fog horns near shore will save you. The three paddled their way through the surf and reached the deeper water of fifty or sixty feet, where the waves were medium sized rollers. If you were prone to sea sickness the motion in this kind ocean might make you sick, but once under, it usually calms down, with a gentle back and forth movement in the deeper water. Throwing up underwater was not something that Robert had experienced. He suspected that if you were sick underwater you could pull your mouth piece out, throw up and then put it back in. You don’t want to get any chunks inside your regulator because it might cause it to malfunction. The divers submerged and went down to about thirty feet. Jim and Gary didn't seem to have any problem clearing their ears. They stayed together and were constantly checking on each other as they observed some very large fish and more of the beautiful underwater scenery.

Scuba Dive Monastery Beach

The Monterey Canyon, one of the most extensive canyon systems in the world, runs along Monterey Bay. And the Canyon is still growing as strong water currents wear away large amounts of sediments to create flows of sand and mud that is similar to an avalanche. This canyon runs past Monastery Beach which is named for the Monastery that is located on a hill across Highway 1. Monastery beach is on the edge of the Carmel submarine canyon which drops down to beyond five thousand feet and is one of the few places where divers can reach extremely deep water, yet still be close to shore.

Monastery beach has one of Monterey's best kelp forests, maybe right up there with any in the world. Though many refer to them as kelp beds, and they do look like lifeless beds if you look at them from a distance as they lay on the surface of the ocean with little activity except for the ocean waves pushing them around. Some may even think that it is gobs of dead plants that have drifted from some South Pacific Island and they may even be seen as an eyesore that interferes with the beauty of the Monterey Peninsula. But, if you have or had the opportunity to dive under the canopy of plants that make up the kelp bed, then you would agree that it's much more than a kelp bed. It is an underwater forest much like trees in a forest on land. The long giant kelp stalks reach down to as deep as one hundred feet, much like a trunk on a tree, as their leaf-like kelp blades float near or on the surface. The kelp forests are only visible to those willing to brave the cool water with scuba equipment. As you enter the forest you see the giant kelp coming up from where it attaches to rocks on the bottom. The kelp blades float on or near the surface to feed on the nutrients of the sea, and like a forest on the land, provide a shelter for birds and animals and a home for fishes, invertebrates and algae. And marine birds and marine mammals find comfortable homes and shelters from the often hostile ocean. The divers knew that the California kelp forests were spectacular but didn't realize that they were the some of the best in the world. Giant kelp thrives in Monterey Bay because this bay has the rocky surfaces that the kelp requires for attaching its roots, and the cool ocean water contains great amounts of nutrients required to sustain the kelp. Kelp uses holdfasts, similar to fingers to grip rocks. Rising from the holdfast are tangled thickets of tough, elastic stripes, which form the scaffolding for the leaf-like kelp blades in which photosynthesis produces food for the plant. Given the proper conditions, growth of a giant kelp frond can exceed a foot per day.

As you approach the beach from Highway 1, you notice is that the beach has a slope much greater than most beaches because it has to match up to the canyon wall that slopes at an angle of about seventy degrees. Submarine canyons are prominent within Monterey Bay and similar in size to the Grand Canyon. As the divers approached the beach, they noticed a huge driftwood tree about two feet in diameter and fifteen feet long that was probably thrown up there like a twig during recent storms, reminding them what the ocean surf can do. But today the breakers on the beach are less than two feet which wasn't too bad considering what they had seen before. Getting in and out of the water is generally interesting, and you don't turn your back on the breakers too long or you'll be taken down.

The divers roamed the forest until their air ran low and then headed for shore. After they returned to the beach and removed their tanks and wetsuit jackets, they watched a diver, who appeared to be by himself, returning to shore. As the diver was close to the beach and standing up, they saw he was carrying a spear gun with something on the end of it. As he faced the beach and started walking to shore, a wave struck his back and knocked him down. He was struggling to get up so the three of them ran down to assist him. Once down, with the heavy tank on his back and the surf continually attacking, he wasn't making any progress getting up. The divers waded in, grabbed his arms, and pulled him to his feet. He started yelling, "My spear gun. Where the hell is my spear gun? What'd you do with my spear gun?" The divers were puzzled with his attitude of implying that they had his spear gun, yet they started searching for it in the sandy water with their bare feet and finally, Gary did feel it with his foot, reached down and picked it up. Fortunately, he picked up the right end, for the spear end held a squirming and angry moray eel. The lone diver, who was now standing and beyond the reach of the surf, rudely grabbed the spear gun from Gary, turned and walked away from him and started to walk up the beach. Gary reached out and grabbed the ungrateful bastard, who was now on the steep slope, and started pulling him back.

Jim said, “What you doing, Gary?”

Gary, madder than Jim had ever seen him, “I’m gonna throw him back.”

Jim looked confused and said, “The eel?”

Gary, very determined, “No, the diver.”

Jim and Robert held their laughter, as they pulled Gary back allowing the now frightened diver to go on his way. The divers returned to their equipment and Gary still very angry, said, “That bastard. Why kill a moray eel?”

Jim nodded and said, “Sounds somebody could use a beer.”

Gary forced a smile, "Well, yeah, I guess that would help." Robert and Jim laughed and finally Gary settled down.

Darker Side of Monastery Beach

The Plymouth’s speedometer indicated a little over seventy five, which was effortless for the V-8 engine, and though seventy-five wasn’t really that fast, it was faster than Gary usually drove. It seemed to Robert that Gary’s grip on the steering wheel was a little overkill but it matched his speed and attitude. Gary just seemed more determined today and more intense to get where he was going in a heck of a hurry. And for the first time since they had been diving together, not all of the divers were in the car and it seemed somewhat strange. Jim was on vacation with his parents. His dad suggested that he go with them because it might be the last time he would see his grandfather, and Jim was okay with that. Not that it was really an option. The two divers in the Plymouth hadn't discussed where they would dive today, but they both seemed to know that this was the day to get the obsession that had been hanging over their heads out of the way. Gary seemed more determined than Robert, but he too knew it had to be completed and put to sleep. And it was something he could have done by himself but he really wasn't a risk taker. He didn't want to die while diving and having people think of him as an ignorant diver that would go off by himself and do something somewhat risky and stupid.

Passing up the beauty of the giant forest of bullwhip kelp anchored to the bottom on rocks sometimes over a hundred feet down, made little sense. But the beautiful underwater forest was not on their minds today. As mentioned before, there are some things in life that you have to do, and the dark side of Monastery Beach offered the solution to quench that thirst, for this was the perfect place for a deep dive. It was perfect place for descending to the deepest depth that was still considered safe using regular compressed air and a single scuba tank. Dive books recommended staying above one hundred feet, but one hundred and twenty feet was the absolute deepest that a diver should descend with a single tank. The deeper you go when breathing compressed air the more air is used. At fifty feet you have about thirty minutes of underwater time, whereas you only have about ten minutes of air at one hundred and twenty feet. Since you only have ten minutes of air left when you reach one hundred and twenty feet, you should immediately start for the surface so you still have enough air left to slowly ascend. A deep dive may be considered by some, a senseless endeavor and a waste of a good tank of air, for as you go to greater depths, there is less sunlight and usually less sea life to observe. Wreck divers are often deep water divers with a sensible reason to go deep and they use dual or triple tanks. One must conclude that this is merely an ego trip for Gary and Robert, but they won't go there more once. Well, unless one of them feels the need to update their self-worth.

Deeper dives have two main hazards, which are decompression sickness and nitrogen narcosis. The divers didn't have to worry too much about decompression because with a single tank of air they wouldn't be breathing compressed air long enough for it to be a major problem. However, even with a single tank it is still important to not ascend too quickly. Air is comprised of about twenty-one percent oxygen and seventy-eight percent nitrogen. Normally, when we breathe the air around us, the lungs can handle both the oxygen and nitrogen gases. However, when a diver breathes compressed air for a long period of time, the lungs cannot handle the larger volume of nitrogen. As a diver descends, the body converts the nitrogen to a solution that is temporarily stored in the blood stream. As the diver starts an accent, the body needs enough time for the nitrogen that was stored in the blood stream to be converted back to a gas. If a diver ascends too quickly the nitrogen will come out of solution in the tissues and blood stream rather than in the lungs and form gas bubbles which may cause decompression sickness. Decompression sickness symptoms can be a rash, breathing difficulty, burning in the chest, muscle pain, dizziness, paralysis, temporary blindness, convulsions, or even unconsciousness if the blockage is in the brain. Yeah, it can kill you.

Though decompression sickness would most likely not be a problem for the divers today, nitrogen narcosis could be a concern because it affects divers differently. The deepest Robert had been was eighty feet and Jim and Gary dropped down to sixty feet one day. It wasn't really a coincidence that Robert and Gary picked today for their deep dive. They thought it was safer if just two of them made this dive because it is easier to keep track and observe one person rather than having a third to deal with. In fact, diving with three had always been a concern of Robert's because of the tractability. Robert, for no logical reason, other than a feeling, thought that Jim might be more susceptible to nitrogen narcosis than Gary or himself. He hadn't mentioned this thought to Gary. Nitrogen narcosis is not quite as understood as decompression sickness because everybody is affected differently and at different depths. Some have more tolerance than others from having this narcosis. Since air contains nearly seventy-eight percent nitrogen, divers have to be aware that high-pressure nitrogen has a narcotic effect on humans. It can cause a sense of euphoria, paranoia, well being, nervousness, and slowing down or dulling of normal functions of the brain and body. Symptoms can be very mild at first and then increase as the diver goes deeper. When affected by high pressure nitrogen, a diver may have difficulty doing things that would normally be easy, such as reading and interpreting instruments, making decisions, or communicating with a buddy. Nitrogen narcosis can cause dizziness or disorientation, and disorientation could cause a diver to go deeper thinking that he is going toward the surface. And if the diver continues to descend then eventually he would become unconscious. The depth which symptoms occur cannot be precisely determined. Many divers will not report any recognizable symptoms of narcosis on dives shallower than sixty to eighty feet, though in clinical studies, divers have shown lack of motor control and slowed cognitive processing as shallow as twenty feet. Nitrogen narcosis is one of the main reasons that it is recommended that recreational divers stay above one hundred feet. But, it's sort of like climbing a mountain or driving a car above a hundred miles per hour. For Robert and Gary going to one hundred and twenty feet was something they had to get out of their system even though many divers, particularly professional divers, wouldn't have an appreciation of the accomplishment.

They opened the trunk, and before suiting up checked their tank pressures and both had a little over 2,700 pounds. Then they suited up and put on their tanks and weight belts. With facemasks, snorkels, and fins in hand, they start walking down the sharply sloped beach. They put on and adjusted their masks and watched the two foot high breakers on the beach and waited for a wave to return to the sea and made a run for the water to get out to a place that was about ten feet deep and put on their fins. Then they quickly paddled out beyond the breakers using their snorkels to conserve air. Once they were away from most of the surf action, they slowly snorkeled and propelled themselves toward the sea. Viewing the bottom as they snorkeled out, suddenly it was as though bottom they had been looking at disappeared. They looked at each and nodded as they replaced the snorkel with their regulator mouthpieces. Each inhaled and exhaled and gave the okay sign. They adjusted their masks and started the dive along the steep canyon wall. The wall had many large boulders and rocks and initially the rocks were covered with an assortment of giant and palm kelp, large anemones, sea stars and sea cucumbers that inhabit the shallow area beneath the kelp forest. At about fifty feet the light was still okay providing some sightseeing as Gary pointed out some volcano and cobalt sponges and Robert pointed to a small lingcod near a large rock and there were numerous rockfish among the nooks and crannies as they passed sixty feet. They normally saw large Medusa jellyfish and ocean sunfish in this area but none today.

As the divers dropped below eighty feet, the rocks were encrusted with various small sea cucumbers and sponges and Gary pointed to some rock scallops that were nested in a crevice. As they descended beyond ninety feet the scenery was losing its luster and becoming quite drab. They started concentrating more on diving than looking for sea life, which speeded up their descent and one hundred feet came quickly. They started looking at each other more frequently to see signs of nitrogen narcosis. Then they started concentrating more on their depth gauges as the gauge needle reached one hundred ten feet and finally one hundred twenty feet. Robert felt shivers, both from the colder water at this depth and perhaps some from knowing he had accomplished the mission. They were there. They reached their goal. Robert looked at Gary's face mask and nodded toward the surface with a questionable look.

But Gary appeared to not understand or had another idea. He grabbed his slate and wrote, "10 more." There was no question mark on the slate. This caught Robert off guard and the thought ran through Robert's mind that Gary was starting to become affected by narcosis. But, this wasn't a good time to get into a conversation about it. Robert nodded, thinking that ten more feet didn't make much difference if they did it quickly and started right back up. They continued down, and at one hundred thirty feet, Robert was relieved, for Gary nodded, smiled and gave the okay sign and they started up. Though this was good news to Robert, now his concern was having enough air to get safely to the surface. And they had no way of knowing how much air they had left, which really didn't matter, because it wasn't as though they could stop at a gas station on the way up. Robert's regulator did have a built in feature that was designed to give an additional air supply when a small lever on the regulator was opened, but the lever was not real easy to reach and he had never tried this feature before because he had never let his tank get empty enough to test it. But soon they were at ninety feet with more light peaking through. They were very close to the steep slope as they made their ascent and it was almost as if they were climbing a mountain. As their tanks were getting empty, thus lighter, Robert picked up a rock from the slope and shoved it under the jacket of his suit so he wouldn't have to fight staying down thus helping conserve air. Soon they were at sixty feet and then forty and they slowed their ascent and even stopped for about a minute at thirty feet to make sure their bodies were compensating for shallower depths. Then they continued up and stopped again at twenty feet.

Gary wrote on this slate, "WOW."

Robert smiled and nodded.

Gary grinned. They stopped again at ten feet and stayed there for about two minutes and then looked up as they broke the surface and shifted to their snorkels and paddled to shore. When they reached the beach and got away from the heavy surf that was waiting to attack, Gary said, “Now, I can say I’m a diver.”

Robert smiled, shook his head and said, “You didn’t have to prove that to me. I’ve seen you drink beer.” Gary smiled.

Seeing Alexia Again

Robert had been working for a carpenter after school and Saturdays for the past two years and his boss seemed pleased with his work. He actually got the job because of some carpentry skills he picked up in Montana with his brothers. When his family moved to the small town of Saco, they were having a problem finding a place to live. But there was an empty warehouse that had been partitioned off like a duplex. One end had very small apartment that nobody lived in. A hallway with bathroom separated the larger end of the warehouse that had a kitchen and a very large open area with no partitions. It seemed the perfect place for the family to live because it was across the street from their dad’s business. However, the large open area would require partitions installed for the bedrooms and the building owner, an older widow, wasn’t willing pay to have them installed. Even though the boys’ dad was capable of building partitions, he was much too busy with his new business, so he turned the project over his sons after some initial training. The boys built the necessary partitions with two by fours and then they had to attach drywall to the partitions and finish off the drywall with tape, spackle and paint. The brothers sort of became carpenters and got better as the partitions progressed.

Robert's boss, an older fellow who was thinking about retirement, decided to not work Saturdays, giving Robert the weekends off. And Robert was okay with that, for he managed to save more money than he spent. And a year ago he bought his Chevy, which was four hundred and fifty dollars, from his savings and was paying the insurance and gas. Sundays had become a dive day for Robert and his diving buddies and Saturdays was girlfriend day. Girlfriend day was the day that the two girls took complete control of Gary and Jim's lives.

There were times when Robert was somewhat envious they had built-in dates, but it wasn't a stifling routine that Robert was anxious to get into. Maybe he liked the adventure of the unknown or possibilities, or variety. Or maybe he hadn't found the right girl to take control of his life. Or maybe no girl wanted to take control of his life. Maybe they all had better choices. Yeah, his mind did wander a bit. So on Saturday mornings he helped his mom and dad around the house and yard and later had to figure what he going to do with the remainder of the day. He resisted the temptation to call Nona, for he didn't want to mess up her life, but he was also afraid that if he called her she wouldn't be available. As irrational as it seems, he would consider, "Oh, I can't tonight," a rejection, and a rejection from her would be far worse than any self-pity that he could create for himself. So, he called Lynnette, a very nice girl he had sort of been going out with. She was a pretty girl with reddish hair and a few freckles, quiet, and a year younger than Robert. They generally went to the drive-in theatre for a make-out session, unless it was good movie, but usually they didn't even know the name of the movie when it was over. After the movie they would drag Main Street for a while and then pull into Mel's Drive-In for a coke and watch the custom cars with big engines and Tijuana upholstery, sewn with American thread because Mexican thread was thought to be inferior, cruise in and out. But he didn't call Lynnette very often during the week and seldom put much thought into calling her ahead of time. And this system had been working fine as far as Robert was concerned, but this Saturday when he called, she said she couldn't go because had to wash her hair. No, it wasn't the first girl that he had known that had hair so dirty that it would take hours to wash. It irritated him and wasn't much of an ego builder, but at the same time, he didn't blame her.

So sometimes he was envious of Jim and Gary who had steady girlfriends, but it wasn't in him to really want that. It was as though he needed the freedom of not knowing what a day would bring. It's similar to gambling. You don't know what the cards will be. Maybe it is the unknown of what is on the other side of that mountain. You could settle down in a safe place at the base of the mountain, but are you always going to wonder what's on the other side? Robert worked hard at keeping the physical part of his life simple, but obviously, he had problems keeping the mental workings of his mind in a simple state. But, "I have to wash my hair," was a clue, particularly since this was the second time in a row that Lynnette had dirty hair. Actually, it was much more than a clue. It was evident that it was time to move on. Unfortunately, he had no backup or substitute for Lynnette.

So whenever he felt down or rejected or lonely, or all three, he loaded his diving equipment into his Chevy. The Monterey Highway always provided some mental peacefulness for him because it was a nice drive. As he cruised along about seventy, the AM station was playing, a Bobby Daren song, "Every night I hope and pray, a dream girl will come my way." He parked on street near the Coast Guard Pier among the abandoned canneries. Some may wonder if John Steinbeck would be disappointed if he saw how the closed canneries looked, as they stood deteriorated from lack of attention. But, perhaps not, for at least they looked peaceful, and appeared to be taking a well-deserved rest, similar to older people that have worked all of their lives and are sitting out on their front porch in a rocking chair contemplating their lives. Most of the old canneries had a next door neighbor, so they weren't alone as they enjoyed the silence after years of a very hectic, but exciting life, as they rested peacefully.

In his haste to get away from Salinas, he had forgotten to put his swimsuit on, so he had to do the towel trick when he removed his jeans and underwear and slipped on his wetsuit trousers, even though there didn't seem to be anybody in sight. The icy water seemed to take its time warming up after submerging, but the water was calm, with excellent visibility. As he snorkeled, he kept an eye on the sea lions that were basking in the sun along the pier, and they kept an eye on him. In particular, the six to eight hundred pound males, who didn't appreciate people messing around their territory or harems. Though they could be very dangerous, there were times, when he had been body surfing, that a sea lion would join him on the wave. The first time it happened, it was quite shocking because he thought it was a shark, but the whiskers and ears gave it away. He considered it an honor when a sea lion joined him on a wave, for they seem to accept you as a friend or playmate, or more likely checking to see if you had speared a fish that he or she could take. He made several dives down to about twenty feet, trying to stay down as long as possible, by concentrating on the spectacular scenery and fish around the rocks, for when you have something like that for distraction, you forget about breathing. And forgetting about breathing is fine as long as you remember that you need air to return to the surface. He liked snorkeling, because it was more challenging than using scuba equipment and it fit better into his struggle for simplicity.

Then he thought about the rule of not diving alone. He always thought it puzzling that pioneer-type individuals like Jacques Cousteau started developing under water breathing devices and doing innovative things and then eventually someone comes along and makes a list of rules. Yes, a list of do's and don'ts that may even become laws once the government finds out because it is an easy agenda item to work on, giving the illusion of doing something important. And at the same time enables one to avoid tackling the difficult important problems. And the person making the rules may not even be directly associated or knowledgeable of the topic. Then somebody figures out how to make money by selling a book or equipment. But, that's capitalism, which Robert felt made the United States the great country that it is. And, nobody forces people to buy the books or equipment that companies sell. Robert had an internal chuckle, thinking someday he might go into the dive shop and they will refuse to fill his tank because he doesn't have a diving license.

He had been out about hour when he headed back to the beach and up to his car. He removed his wetsuit and put on his jeans and a T-shirt and then noticed a familiar looking truck that had not been there when he went into the water. He took a deep breath of ocean air and looked over at the sea lions, still basking in the sun and it appeared that they were having a relaxing day. Though he didn't know what they were thinking, it probably wasn't a concern that they would soon need a license to bask in the sun. He looked away from the sea lions and across the street and saw a woman getting out of the truck. It was the women they helped. Her named slipped his mind for a few seconds and then he remembered that it was Alexia. At that moment, he was glad that Lynnette's hair was dirty and he wished her well, for she was a nice girl, but this was like getting dealt the right hand, which for Robert, when dealing with girls, had not happened that often. The woman had more furniture and boxes in the bed of her truck. But then he realized something, causing his enthusiasm to dwindle, because when they met her before, Gary had driven his Plymouth, so she wouldn't recognize his car. And now he was wishing Jim was here. Yeah, gregarious Jim would be waving and already walking over there to talk to her. That wasn't something he could do. But suddenly, she started waving. He looked around to see if there was anyone else on the street. Maybe she was merely a friendly person that waved at all strangers, for he couldn't imagine that she remembered him. Then he was further surprised when she started walking across the street toward him. Robert is stupidly stunned as he watches this beautiful woman, who he and his diving buddies had estimated to be about twenty-four or twenty-five, and definitely knew, without estimating, that she had a great body. And the closer she came, the prettier she got.

She smiled and said, “Hi. It's Robert, right?”

Robert stammered a bit, “Yeah that’s right. And you're Alexia.”

She nodded and continued, “Where’s your friends?"

“Well they sort of deserted me for the day. They both have girlfriends.”

She said in a very surprised manner, “You don’t have a girlfriend?”

“Well, there is this girl that I sometimes go out with, but she had to wash her hair.”

Alexia smiled, nodded and said, “I see.”

Robert shrugged, smiled and then said, “Well, you know how important washing your hair is. It’s right up there with having your appendix taken out.” Alexia laughed. Robert continued, “So here I am. But I think this is where I belong.”

Alexia said, “Well, I’m sure if you had wanted a date, you could have found one.”

He shrugged and said, “I suppose. How’s the place coming along?”

She sort of put her teeth together, clenched her jaw and nodded very slowly as though she was negotiating some answering time, and finally said, “Pretty good. There are times when I think I’m completely nuts. There are other times, when I’m depressed for living here or trying to live here, but then I realize that I can’t imagine living anywhere else. I’ve never been one to take the easy route. I come home in the evening, get into my jeans and sweatshirt and old tennis shoes and walk along the beach, every day regardless of the weather. For me, even a bad day down here is nice. Want to come up and take another look at the place?"

Robert was very surprised and stumbled his words a bit, "Oh, sure, yeah, I’d like that.”

Alexia said, “But you have to promise not to expect too much. The changes are quite subtle. Everything will take time and money. You'll just have to use your imagination, as I do.”

He looked at a large box in the truck and said, “Want this taken up?”

"Oh, that'd be great. Thanks." He grabbed the box and followed her up the metal stairs trying hard, but not entirely successfully, to not stare at her womanly ass. He really didn’t remember paying much attention to Lynnette’s ass.

She said, “There's also a stairway inside the cannery to the loft, but the cannery still has that fishy odor. I’ve thought about building some rooms in the cannery area and renting them out if I could get rid of that odor.”

Robert said, “I think the fish smell is part of the atmosphere. You could actually charge more because of it.”

She laughed and said, “You might have something there.” Then she laughed again said, “No really. Advertising never seems to be based on logical thinking. The ad could be something like, only a few units left that have the original odor from the Doc Rickets and Steinbeck era.”

“Doc Rickets?”

“Oh, no. Don’t tell me. You haven’t read Cannery Row?”

He felt foolish when he had to say, “No, I haven’t.”

“Well, that'll be your first assignment. You'll appreciate the book because of the amount of time you spend over here."

Alexia unlocked the metal door, and the hinges creaked as she slowly opened it. Robert was thinking about the can of WD-40 in his car.

“Now, promise not to laugh.”

Robert, with a very straight face, "Oh, I can't promise that." She laughed.

They entered the large open space and he said, “Wow, it’s starting to look like a home.”

“Yeah, finally got my furniture. The little I have anyway. It’s challenging trying to make a home out of a factory office area. I’ve arranged the furniture where rooms would be." He looked over at a large bed in the far corner along with bedroom furniture and then an area next to it that had another bed with a nightstand and lamp.

“Now, you have to imagine there are walls. As you can see, I’ve marked off with masking tape where the rooms will be and where the doors are. So be careful you don’t walk through a wall.” Robert laughed. She continued, “It helps if you remember the story about the emperor having no clothes.” At least Robert knew that story so he didn’t have a dumb look on his face when he laughed again. She said, “Okay, let me show you around the place. I know you've been here before but that's before I had furniture and the imaginary walls."

The kitchen had a sink, a small stove and countertop. Her grandfather spent a lot of time in his office, so it was equipped with a coffee pot and some kitchen items. A very sturdy round table with four chairs separated the kitchen from the living room. The oak table had been her grandfather's. Her living room had a small sofa and a large round coffee table that looked rugged enough to sit on. A large comfortable looking leather chair sat in the corner of the room with an end table and a lamp for reading.

She raised her eyebrows in a seductive manner, or what seemed seductive to Robert, and said, "Want to see my bedroom?"

Robert hesitated before answering, "I guess."

The only time he had ever been invited into a girl's bedroom was when he was twelve years old. A classmate's thirteen year old sister agreed to show her nude body and then kiss Robert and his friend Keith. Keith had arranged the event with the girl's brother. And Keith made the most of his view of the naked sister as she lay on her bed. But, when Robert looked into the girl's eyes, he sensed sadness and could not go any further down her body. But even if he hadn't perceived her to be sad, he couldn't have looked at her body, for it didn't seem right. After she dressed she put her arms around Keith and gave him his first kiss. After a short time, she pulled away from Keith, who was very proud, with a satisfied look on his face and gave the impression that he could now check that off his to do list.

She started to put her arms around Robert, but he timidly backed away. Then she smiled at him, a very caring and understanding smile, gently took his hand, guided him into her closet and shut the door. As they faced each other, she slowly put her arms around him, lightly pressed her cheek against his, and whispered, "It's okay." He relaxed and moved against her, and she held him, initially with a mother-like tenderness, but as they held each other, it seemed her role had shifted, as an emotion, a stirring that was peaceful, natural, with a touch of yearning came over her. It was a feeling that she had never experienced before, and didn't want it to end, but forced herself to gently pull away, for she didn't want to scare him and destroy what seemed to be, a magical moment. A moment that would stay with her as a measure of what a relationship is really about.

She had tears in her eyes and said, “Thank you, Robert.” He looked puzzled, not understanding why she said that, for he felt like a failure for not kissing her, but was glad he didn’t look at her body. He never let Keith know that he did not look at her or kiss her. If Keith had known, he probably would have tried to get back some of the dollar that he had paid the brother. But, what Robert did not know, was that this was the last time the sister displayed her body.

As Robert stood outside the pretend walls, Alexia watched him for a while and finally said, “What are you thinking about?”

He shook his head and said, “Oh, nothing." Then he stammered a bit and said, “It was something that happened a long time ago.”

She said, “Well, I have a good memory, and I’ll get the story out of you someday.” Then she reached through the pretend bedroom doorway, grabbed his hand, and pulled him in. She said, “Don’t worry, I’ll be gentle.” She laughed and he smiled as they went in. The room had two medium sized windows that had all the possibilities of a spectacular view of the bay that was directly below the windows. You could even hear the surf crashing against the rocks below. However, the windows, with years of accumulating soot, salt, and specks of at least three different colors of paint, made looking through them impossible.

She said, “It’s a good thing they’re so dirty since I don’t have any window coverings. Course a peeping tom would need a fifty foot ladder.”

He remembered reading a story about the actress, Kim Novak, who at one time had a house right on the coast between Carmel and Big Sur. Her house sat on a cliff that overlooked the ocean. Her bathroom had a large picture window above her bathtub. Nobody could look into the window because of the steep cliff below, but the actress said that some brave pilots in small planes would on occasion fly along the cliff at the same level as her window for a possible peek.

Alexia moved toward the window, leaned into it with her face nearly touching, and said, “If you stand real close you can see that the view isn’t too bad.” He nodded as he stood admiring her ass. “Come and take a look.” He moved to the window and stood next to her as she cupped her hands around her face, even though it didn’t help much. Their shoulders touched and he moved away a little, not that he wanted to move away, he just didn’t want to give her the wrong impression. But even without touching he could still feel the warmth from her body. And he wondered how someone could smell so nice even after they had been hauling boxes and moving furniture.

He said, “It’s a nice view all right. If you ever sell the place you can advertise it as having an ocean view if you stand real close to the window.” She laughed. They turned and faced each other.

Robert said, “You know, I could wash those windows for you.”

"Are you crazy?”

Robert looked at her very seriously, and with a straight face said, “Most people don’t find that out until at least the second day of being around me.”

She laughed and then, with an inquisitive look said, “How would you wash those windows?”

Robert looked at the window casing that had been painted shut, and not opened for some time and noticed that the metal slider frame had four screws on each side.

He said, “If I take out these Phillip head screws and break that paint seal I should be able to take the bottom part of the window out. Once it is removed, I can reach out and clean the upper part.”

“So you'd have to sit on the window sill, with your body outside and reach up and wash the upper window.”

“Yeah.”

She said, “No, I don’t think so.”

"Okay. Let's at least open the lower window."

"I've tried. I couldn't get it open."

"It looks like the paint is holding it. I have some tools in the car if you want me to try."

"Well, it'd be nice to be able to open it." She hesitated and said, "Okay, but are you sure you want to take the time to do this?"

"I'm in no hurry being down on my luck with girls and all." She laughed.

Robert always carried a few basic tools in his car because the car was pushing ten years old and he never knew when he might have to repair it on the road. He even carried a hammer that he used to tap on the starter solenoid to free it up. Actually, his dad taught him that trick. He went down to his car and brought back a tool bag. He used the hammer and screwdriver to chip away some of the old paint that was preventing the window from opening and then with a little jiggling, he was able to slide the window up, and as it went up, a gust of ocean breeze filled the room.

She smiled and in amazement, said, "Wow, what a nice breeze."

Then he said, "You know, it wouldn't be that hard to take that lower window out and at least wash the outside of it."

Again, she hesitated and said, "But what if you can't get it back in?"

"I'm pretty sure that I'll be able to get it back in."

"Well, okay." After removing the four screws from each side of the metal frame and some more jiggling he removed lower window from the frame. He held the window while Alexia used a bucket of soapy water and a rag to remove the first coat of grime. And then she used a razor blade to remove years of paint specks and drips.

She said, "I wonder if this window has ever been washed on the outside?"

"Doesn't look like it, does it?"

After she removed the first layer of grime and paint, she used Windex and a rag as though she was polishing her finest silver, if she had been a fine silver kind of woman. She noticed Robert was looking at the upper window.

“I know what you are thinking and I don’t like it.”

“It wouldn’t be that difficult. All I have to do is sit on the window sill and reach up. My legs will still be inside and you could hold them so I don’t fall backwards.”

“Oh, no. How do you know I can hold you?”

"We could practice."

She laughed and said, "You mean practice holding you? Boy you are smooth."

Robert laughed and said, "I could sit on this bench and lean back and you can hold my knees."

She nodded and said, "I don't know. Well, okay." But, before she realized it, Robert was sitting on the sill with his legs hanging inside and upper body balanced outside and she frantically made a grab for his legs.

She sighed, looked up and saw he was looking at her through the dirty upper window. He said, “Hi.”

“Damn you. Get back in here. It’s not worth it.”

Then she realized she had her hands quite high on his thigh and gradually eased them down a little making sure she didn’t lose her grasp on him.

He smiled and said, “Well, I’m here now. I might as well wash this window. Hand me the wet rag so I get the first coat off.”

She still looked angry, or maybe upset, but it was almost worth it because he was starting to enjoy her hands on his thighs and the pressure from her lower body against his knees. She reluctantly removed one hand from his thigh and made sure that he was still balancing on the sill and then carefully reached down to grab the wet rag and handed it to him. Then he reached up and wiped the first layer of grime from the window and handed the rag back to her. She rinsed the rag in her bucket of soapy water and handed it back out. They repeated this several times until he had removed the first layer of soot, salt, and grime. Robert was feeling quite comfortable sitting on the ledge thinking he was doing a high wire act and continued to like the feel of her hands. He asked for the razor blade to remove the paint specks. She stretched to reach the razor blade and for a couple seconds, let go of his legs completely, but he was able maintain his balance. He appeared to be enjoying himself, and was able to show off a little without it being too obvious. He felt quite comfortable as she handed him the Windex and a clean rag for the final cleaning of the window. They looked at each other through the clean window, and she stuck her tongue out at him. He smiled and said, “See anything we missed?”

“No, I want you back in here right now.”

He pulled himself into the room and he was thinking she might hit him. But instead she hugged him and said, “Don’t ever do anything like that again.” She released him, stood back and looked through the clean upper window. Then she looked at him smiled, and said, “But it does look nice.”

Robert replaced the lower window and the screws that held the frame. Then he sprayed the window guide with WD-40 that was also in his tool bag, and moved the window up and down a few times until it operated smoothly. Alexia looked at Robert as though he was a surgeon that had just completed a complex operation. Now with the comparison of the clean window with the dirty window, Alexia knew she had no choice. She just shook her head, rolled her eyes and reluctantly gave in and let him clean it. The clean windows were now wide open and the ocean air was filling the entire loft with probably more fresh air than the loft had felt in twenty years.

It was nearly lunch time and Alexia was enjoying her new view of Monterey bay when she said, “I’d like to buy you lunch. There's a place on the wharf that has really good fish sandwiches. You like fish?”

He said, “Yeah, I like fish, but you don’t have buy me lunch. I should be going.”

She said, “Look, when you insisted on washing the windows, you said you weren't in a hurry. But I guess it must be boring hanging around an old woman.”

Robert shook his head and said, “Oh no, I just don’t want you to think that you owe me anything. This has been a fun day for me. I mean working with you and everything.”

“Come on, let’s wash up and go to lunch.” Robert just nodded.

They started walking down Cannery Row and Alexia said, “Did you know that this street was originally called, Ocean View Avenue?”

Robert said, “No, no, I didn’t.”

“Yeah, it was renamed after Steinbeck wrote the Cannery Row book.”

As they walked slowly past the deserted canneries, some more dilapidated than others, Alexia said, “This guy named Frank E. Booth owned a cannery in Sacramento and for a few years, he shipped the salmon caught in Monterey to Sacramento. I guess that's a couple hundred miles. But, in 1902, he opened the first real cannery in Monterey. He called it the “Monterey Packing Company.” Robert was taking in what she saying, but when her arm would accidentally brush against his arm, it would sort of sidetrack his mind. Then she continued, “I hope I don’t bore with Monterey history, but since we’re here, I can pass on things my grandfather told me.”

Robert said, “Wait a minute. I thought you were just taking me to lunch. You didn’t say anything about history lessons.”

Alexia laughed and said, “Just pay attention. You’d be surprised what you might learn from me.” They looked at each other briefly and Alexia smiled.

Robert sensed she was embarrassed by what she had just said, so he quickly asked, “Why was the original cannery a salmon cannery? I thought they canned sardines here?”

Alexia said, “So, you know more than you let on. Although, that’s a good question, you're getting ahead of the lesson. We're gonna get to that. I won’t have you speed up my presentation."

"Sorry."

"Well, remember Frank Booth, who started the first cannery. Well, he hired an Italian guy named Knut Hovden to manage this cannery. Hovden had been in the fishing industry in Italy and brought fishing techniques and his canning inventions from Italy.”

While listening to Alexia, Robert was thinking that this was the best history lesson that he had ever had. The inventions and techniques actually did have his interest and he had always enjoyed the atmosphere of Cannery Row so the history was becoming more interesting.

“What kind of inventions?”

“Well, one was a machine used to solder cans shut and another was the purse bottom nets that were used to haul the sardines from the boats to shore. And then Hovden hired Pietro Ferrante, another Italian, who had invented the *lampara* net. I don’t know why, but *lampara* nets were very reliable and were more efficient at catching fish. As they fished for salmon they soon realized that sardines were more plentiful than salmon. That’s when Booth’s Monterey Canning Company, starting canning sardines.”

Robert said, "And that’s when others started building canneries?"

"Yeah, eventually there were thirty canneries in Monterey. And they canned sardines for nearly fifty years."

Alexia was not out of history lessons, but they had arrived at Wharf. There were a few visitors, but it was not that busy considering it was a Saturday. They walked to the middle of the wharf and Alexia said, “It’s right here.”

They ordered their sandwiches at the counter and then waited for the order to come up. After about ten minutes they had hot fish sandwiches wrapped in a brown paper and carried them to an outside table. Robert went back for the two cokes that they had also ordered. The round table was quite small causing their knees to brush several times, as they unwrapped and ate their sandwiches.

Alexia said, "Really, if I start boring you with the history stuff, just tell me to shut up. It's just that I don't get a chance a chance to talk about it much. Most of the people I associate with would rather talk about themselves. Many are intellectual snobs, who look down upon about everybody including each other. And they live in what they call New Monterey or on the 17-Mile Drive. You know where the million dollar homes are. Many of them think of Cannery Row as a slum, just as many of their parents and grandparents did when the canneries were operating. And now, there are many second generation families that live off the wealth their parents worked to create. So, they too, are living off the wealth that was generated from these canneries."

Robert said, "No, you're not boring me. I'm enjoying this."

Alexia continued, "And I'm not saying that I'm too much better than the intellectual snobs, for I don't strike up a conversation with the occasional hobo or bum that I see in this area, even though they are my neighbors. Some have even offered me swig of whatever they have in those brown paper bags. Not that I'm not tempted at times."

Robert laughed and said, "Any chance we might get lucky and run into one those hobos on the way back? I wouldn't mind a drink right now."

Alexia laughed and said, "In the early nineteen hundreds, Monterey was becoming a tourist attraction. That's when they built the Del Monte Hotel. So between the money made from the canneries and the tourists discovering the beauty of the entire area, Monterey started to grow. Since most of the people that I associate with live in New Monterey, there is never a danger of them seeing me on Cannery Row. They'd sooner be seen in a second hand store than venture onto my street." They continued eating their sandwiches and enjoying the ocean air. She said, "Been a long time since I've talked so much. And I didn't even give you a chance to talk."

"That's okay. I'm not much of a talker."

She smiled "Well, I appreciate your help today. Being able to see though those windows gives me hope. There were days when I stared at the imaginary walls and thought I was in over my head. But now I have an ocean view."

Robert said, “You know, I could build your walls for you.”

She looked at him in amazement, disbelief, or both, and said, “Really?”

He nodded and said, “Yeah.”

“You've put in a wall before?”

He said, “Yeah, when we lived Saco, Montana, my brothers and I built walls in an old warehouse that our family lived in.”

“You lived in Montana?” She nodded and continued, “You lived in Montana in an old warehouse?”

Robert nodded and said, “Yeah, Saco had several old large houses but they all had widowed women living in them, and some of the women ran rooming houses, but there wasn't any place big enough for our family to live. The warehouse location was perfect because it was across the street from my dad's new business.”

She said, “I have never heard of Saco, Montana.”

“How many cities have you heard of in Montana?”

She said, “Helena, it's the capital, and then there's Billings, and well, you know, I don't know. I think Montana is one those states that only has two towns, just Helena and Billings.” Robert laughed. “How long did you live in this place you call, Saco?”

“Three years. My dad had an International Harvester Agency there”

"Okay, suppose that I actually believed there is a Saco in Montana and you lived there. How old were you then?"

He said, "I was in the third grade when we moved there."

She said, "So you were maybe nine years old. At nine years old you learned how build a wall."

"My dad was the kind of person that could do anything. And I didn't even realize it at the time, but he was an excellent teacher and with an older brother the information sort trickled down. My dad or older brother apparently didn't underestimate our abilities even though to most people we might have been considered young. I don't know if my dad thought of himself as a teacher, but he did know that he didn't have time to build the walls himself so he showed us boys how to do it and then he was able to concentrate on the business. My two brothers and I built six walls to make the warehouse into a place to live. Actually, they were partitions and that's what yours would because they don't support a roof. And now, I work part time for a carpenter who builds houses."

"Okay, so suppose I believe that you know how to install walls or partitions. You don't have time to do that with a part time job and all. Do you?"

"I have weekends off and partitions actually go up pretty fast."

"What about bedroom doors? You do that too?"

He said, "Yeah, you can buy the door frame with the door and then you space the wall studs out so the door frame fits into the wall as you build it."

"You really wanna do this?"

"You seem easy enough to work with."

She smiled and said, "Okay, but no more high wire acts."

"I was just trying to impress you."

She said, “You impressed me the first time I saw you even before you said anything. All you did was stand there." Robert had a puzzled look but said nothing. They walked back to the cannery and Alexia excitedly took out a notebook of large graph paper with penciled plans that looked to have been modified several times, and laid them out on the table. The drawings were quite clear and it was obvious that she had put a lot of thought into them. Using the plans, he measured the areas where the walls were needed. Robert had enough information to determine the lumber, hardware, doors and drywall that was required to frame and drywall the walls for the two bedrooms. They decided that Alexia could order the materials and have them delivered during the week and they could start installing them on Saturday.

She said, “Isn’t this going to interfere with your diving?”

He said, “It shouldn't take long to frame the rooms and get the drywall up. I can come over early Saturday Morning. Would eight o’clock be too early?"

Then Alexia seemed upset and said, “Robert, one problem is, I have, or the thing is, that I have a friend. When I came to Monterey I had to take courses for my California teaching credential. He was the professor and I didn’t know anybody so when he asked me out, I said yes and things just progressed.” Alexia didn’t know why she felt she had to explain this to Robert.

Then she continued, “And we have plans for dinner next Friday and sometimes after we go out, we...”

He cut her off and said, “No, that’s okay, how about sometime in the afternoon?"

“Well, I might not be here. He won’t be staying with me here. I don’t bring him here. Sometimes we go to his place for the night. He thinks I’m crazy for trying to live here. He said he wasn’t going to spend any time in an oversized sardine can, which could have been quite funny, if he hadn’t been serious.”

“Well, do you have an idea what time you’ll be back on Saturday? I can come when you get back.”

She said, “I’ll give you a key and you can let yourself in on Saturday.”

“Are you sure?”

“Yes, I but I hate for you to have to work alone. And there is another problem." She looked at him apologetically and finally said, "On Saturday afternoon we are supposed to go to a party that starts about four o’clock.”

He said, “If you don’t mind me being here when you’re gone, I can do most of the work by myself.”

She hesitated as though she wasn’t saying exactly what was on her mind, and then said, “I’m not being fair to you, but the party plans have been made for a while.”

Robert suddenly assumed that she really didn't think it was a good idea he work alone or he wasn’t capable of building the partitions and said, “No, that’s okay. Maybe we should put off the walls for a while. Maybe when you are ready you can give me a call. The last thing I want to do is complicate your life. I’ve enjoyed working with you today and the lunch was great. It was a good day for me. I really have to get going.”

“I’m sorry, Robert.” She didn’t know how to stop him from leaving with the wrong impression. She was upset, and it wasn’t that she minded him working by himself. It’s just that she wanted to be able to work with him on the project, but he left before she could explain that to him. He had no way of knowing that this had been the best day that she’d had for a long time. After Robert left, she started crying. She had almost been at this mental state anyway because she had overwhelmed herself with this project. And then destiny gives her a partner to work with and she drove him away.

Calling Nona

It wasn't a fun drive home. Not only did he enjoy working with her, he knew he would have enjoyed the project. It had been a long time since he'd had something like this to do. He decided to call Nona even though he told her he wouldn't, but as he was making the call, he almost wished that she didn't answer because he had interfered with enough lives for one day. The phone rang twice and he then he decided he would give it one more ring.

As the third ring started he heard, "Hello."

He was silent for a few seconds and said, "Hi, Nona."

"Oh, Robert, are you okay?"

"Oh sure, I just wanted talk to you. Be okay if I come over?"

She hesitated and said, "Well I sort of have plans and I have to go out. I'm sorry. I didn't expect you to call."

"That's okay. I promised I wouldn't call. It wasn't a good idea. I don't mean to interfere."

He started to hang up the phone when she said, "No, I'm glad you called. Look, I'll be home by ten. Can you come over then?"

"Ten, oh no, that's crazy. I don't want to disturb your parents and I don't even know what I want to talk about. I'd probably sit there and say nothing."

She laughed and said, "I like it when you say nothing. And well, my parents are out of town. Maybe we can think of something that doesn't require talk. Please come over."

"Are you sure?"

"I'm sure."

As he drove toward Nona’s house, reservations plagued his mind. What if her parents happened to come home earlier than expected? What if her neighbors see him going into the house? But soon the Chevy was on her street, and though he considered parking around the corner from her house so her neighbors wouldn’t get the wrong idea, he went ahead and parked along the curb in front of her house, hurried to her front door and knocked lightly.

When Nona opened the door, Robert was stunned, for she was wearing a long dark blue robe, and a scent of a very pleasurable soap radiated from her entire body, making it obvious that she had just gotten out of the shower. She took his hand, led him into the house and locked the door. They faced each other and hugged.

She said, "I missed you."

"I missed you too. I wanted to call but I promised I wouldn't."

She said, "I don't know why we're punishing ourselves." They pulled back a bit from the hug, allowing their cheeks to briefly come together before she turned her head until her lips were on his cheek and then their lips came together, gently at first, and then with much more yearning. She took his hand and guided him to the sofa. As they sat together, she pulled him down on top of her and their lips came together again. They pulled back from their kiss and lay on their sides facing each other.

"I'm glad you're here. Are you okay?"

"Oh, yeah, I'm fine."

"Well, you seem down." She pulled him closer and they hugged. She continued, "Can I ask you something very personal?"

Robert hesitated and then said, "I don't know, sounds scary."

"Yeah it is scary. But aren't you curious?"

"Yeah, I guess."

She said, “Oh, I’d better not ask this. You might think I’m… well, I don’t know what you’ll think.”

“Well, I think you’ve committed yourself.”

Nona said, "Okay, but don’t think I’m a bad person. I was wondering if you have ever had sex.”

Robert shook his head awkwardly, wondering if he should lie about it. He wanted to have the right answer, but he didn’t know the right answer, and finally decided on the truth and said, "No. No, I haven't."

Nona said, "Do you want to know if I have?"

"I don't know. Maybe I don't want to know."

Nona said, "Well, I'll tell you anyway. I haven't either."

Robert, relieved said, "I'm glad."

"I’m glad too. I've thought about it, but I guess everybody has thought about."

He said, "I thought if people were going together for a long time they might."

"I suppose some might, but not Chuck and me. We have more of a friendship relationship. When we’re together we’re surrounded by a group of people. Initially I was caught up in the fun of hanging out with the football crowd. I guess I am sort of using Chuck to be part of what I thought of as a college life style. But, it has kind of lost its luster. And then I met you and now, well, I like being with you.”

Robert said, "I've always enjoyed just making out so I've never tried for anything more, and I don't like to be rejected. So, I try not to put myself in a position where I can be rejected"

"Yeah, you're the kind of guy that would have to be pulled down and taken advantage of."

"That might work, but not without a lot of resistance.”

She laughed and said, “That attitude is in contrast to the way you live. I thought you thrived on taking chances. I mean diving and all."

"I don't think I take many chances. And besides, physical punishment is much easier to take than mental punishment. And girl rejection is the toughest of all."

"I suppose most girls don't have to worry about rejection when it comes to sex. But they do suffer a lot when they hope someone will call and they don't."

He said, "You mean me?"

"No, dummy, I mean the guy with the Chevy that has big tires on the rear, flames on the doors, and the engine that makes a lot of noise."

He laughed and said, "I don't want to cause you any trouble or hurt you."

"Look, when I think the time is right, don't make me have to call the guy with the loud motor."

Robert laughed and said, "To me, a relationship is like unwrapping a Christmas gift. The process should be so slow that you never get it completely unwrapped so you don't use up all of the pleasure."

Nona laughed and said, "Yes opening gifts is scary because you may be disappointed."

"That's true, but I don't think, well, I know, if I unwrapped you completely, I would not be disappointed, but I don't think I would deserve such a nice gift. And I'd be afraid that I may not be able to use it properly."

She laughed and said, "One good thing about certain gifts is that they don't require any assembly so you can concentrate on learning how to use it. Remember the first time you tried to ride a bike? Wasn't it sort of wobbly at first?" He smiled and nodded. She continued, "But even if you tipped over that didn't stop you from getting back on, did it?"

"No, but I never had a new bike that I worried about getting scratched. And the old bike I did have, I shared with my brother."

"Well, it's nice to share things with your brother. But there are some things that probably shouldn't be shared." He nodded and laughed. She pulled his hand to her lips.

He nervously said, "It had a dented fender and the chain was always coming off. And the paint had scratches" He put the back of his hand on her soft cheek. He continued, "So I wasn't so worried about tipping over. But if it had been a new bike, with perfect paint, maybe I would have been worried about scratching it, or riding it wrong so I wouldn't have been able ride it very well."

She gives him a doubtful look, "You know, when you called, you said you weren't gonna talk. You think too much Commando Guy. My paint's not perfect. I have moles and birthmarks and sometimes my face breaks out when I eat French fries."

She kissed him, stood up, took his hand, pulled him to his feet, and then led him upstairs to her bedroom. They stood near her bed and she said, "Would you stay with me tonight? I want you to hold me. We'll keep the gift wrapped for now. We'll just take off this bow." She undid the cloth belt and slipped off her robe, revealing cotton pajamas that were buttoned up to her slender neck. She went to a dresser drawer and pulled out pajama bottoms and said, "Put these on." She sighed as they snuggled together and fell asleep.

Scuba Dive Monastery Kelp Forest

As Jim's Oldsmobile headed toward Monterey, Gary said, "What did you do last weekend, Robert? We are thinking that maybe you and Nona got together. In fact I saw her the other day and she said, "Be sure and say hi to Robert". I think she would dive with us if you asked her."

Robert said, "Maybe we should. She is a nice girl."

Jim said, “Did you go out with her last weekend?”

“No, I don’t want to mess up her life. But, remember the cannery woman?”

Jim said, “Remember her? Jesus, I think about her every night.”

Robert laughed and said, “I went diving last weekend and I saw her. She asked about you guys and she showed me her loft again.”

Jim said, “She took you to her loft? No, I don't believe it.”

“She asked if I wanted to see the progress and I helped her wash some windows.”

Jim pulled the Oldsmobile off into the sand alongside the road near Monastery Beach. Robert was glad they arrived because he didn’t want to answer any more questions about Alexia. He was trying to forget her and Nona too. He needed his simple life back. He needed girl friends that made no difference to him whether they said yes or no when he asked them for a date. He didn't care if they had to wash their hair or take care of their little brother or whatever excuse they used to not go out with him. He wanted to be with girls or women that didn't mean anything to him. Ones that didn’t make him feel bad when they rejected him.

They suited up at the trunk of Jim’s car and after checking the air pressure of the tanks, put the tanks on their backs and walked down the steep beach. The surf was breaking about three feet in the center area of the beach so they entered on the South end where it was not quite as violent. They snorkeled out beyond the surf and to the beginning of the kelp forest. They entered at the edge of the kelp forest, submerged and settled down to about twenty feet and swam into the amazing forest. You could still feel the waves at twenty feet and the kelp swayed back and forth as did the divers, almost in a synchronous dance, as they made their way through the forest trying very hard to not touch or disturb it. Entering the underside of the canopy and surrounded by towering stocks of giant kelp that extend much deeper than the divers are going today, gave the feeling of being in an underwater forest with rays of sunshine seeping through when there was an occasional open space in the canopy. Each time Robert dove here it reinforced his impression that was in this was indeed a kelp forest rather than a kelp bed.

The divers found an area that had a clearing and formed a circle facing each other. Gary held up his writing slate to Robert's face. The slate said, "Why didn't you tell us?"

Robert wrote, "What?"

Jim wrote, "The cannery woman."

Robert wrote, "You wanta dive or talk?" Jim and Gary laughed.

Gary wrote, "Will talk on surface."

They continued on, single file through the kelp forest because it was so thick that it was not possible to travel side by side. But as always, they maintained visual contact with each other. Robert and Gary were particularly careful to keep an eye on Jim because he tended to stray a little too far away. Gary was still the most observant of each nook and cranny and would typically be the one to discover a fish or plant that they had not seen before. If Gary waved you over, you didn't hesitate, for it was always something special. Jim still tended to take in more territory than he could handle and was usually the first to run low on air because of his somewhat hyperactivity. Robert was in between Jim and Gary in detailed observation skills, but had the same air usage as Gary. It always seemed that the diving time here went twice as fast because it was so phenomenal, which also made the icy water seem less noticeable.

As their air ran low, they turned to the south and started out of the kelp forest for a clearing where they could surface and snorkel into the beach. Upon breaking the surface they could see that the surf was stronger than when they went in, which was not uncommon, for it didn't take long for Monterey Bay water to change, generally for the worst. As they snorkeled toward the beach they reached a point where they could wait for an incoming wave and were able to have it carry them into the beach and hope for an easy landing on their feet. Once they hit the sand they hurriedly removed their fins and stood up as the powerful outgoing wave was trying to pull them back in. They broke free of the powerful rushing water and were able to reach higher ground. Again they were able to get out without being taken down by the surf. Every time they dived here they prided themselves on getting out without becoming a victim of the powerful water. Not a fatal victim but taking a few tumbles where they might need help to get up. Carrying a tank, weight belt, fins, and sometimes forgetting to remove buoyancy compensating rocks from inside your wetsuit makes for an easy target for surf that seems intent on taking down anyone or anything that invades its territory.

There's two ways to combat heavy surf; use it to carry you in the direction it wants to go or tantalize it from the safety of the beach with a beer in your hand. Yet, when even safely out of its reach, it seems comparable to a mountain whose steepness tries to keep you from climbing it, but at the same time seductively beckons.

As the divers watched the surf and noticed that it was picking up even more, they were glad they got out when they did. They took off their wetsuit jackets and rested on the beach for a while. Though there weren't any other divers around, there was a family with four kids, all in sweaters, sitting on the beach with a picnic lunch and the kids were looking at the divers and Jim was enjoying the attention. He was becoming quite good at playing the role of a diver and was getting to a point where he was a diver.

Jim said, "Anybody for a beer?" Though the divers were very wary of getting caught drinking, it was almost as though they deserved a beer after taking on the monstrous sea and the day seemed like the kind of day that the police would rather be sitting in a nice warm restaurant drinking coffee and eating donuts. The divers carried their tanks down to the surf, and after some difficulty, they were able to rinse some of the sand off and then they carried them to the car and removed the regulators. Then they returned to the surf with their wetsuits and rinsed them off and took them to the car. Robert and Gary watched for the police as Jim opened the beer and poured each can into paper cups in the seclusion of his open trunk. They carried their cups to the beach and sat down and watched the kids teasing the surf with their feet from a respectable distance, under the very watchful eyes of their parents. The surf, if given a chance, would not show any mercy, for dogs, children or adults.

Gary took a sip of beer, sighed, and said, “Okay, what’s this about the cannery woman?”

Robert said, “Well, I washed some windows for her.”

Jim chuckled, and then wiped away some beer that dribbled down the side of his mouth before saying, “So one day you merely climbed that long set of stairs to her attic house, knocked on the door and said, "Howdy miss, I’m the window washer guy. I happened to be in the neighborhood and I’m here to wash your windows.”

Robert with a surprised look said, “How did you know? That’s it. That’s just how it happened.”

Gary said, “Assuming you did wash her windows, how did you meet up with her again? I still think that you and Nona have something going and you are trying to cover it up with this cannery women story.”

Robert smiled and said, “A few weeks ago, a Saturday I think, you both had dates and I tried to get one with Lynnette, but she had to wash her hair. You know how dirty her hair gets when I happen to call. Anyway, I felt sorry for myself for a while, and then I did what I do best. I went diving.”

Jim said, “You went diving by yourself. What kind of example is that for your students?” Robert nodded and smiled.

Gary said, “So you went diving and then what?”

“I had finished the dive and was getting my wetsuit off and noticed her truck across the street. And then she waved and walked toward me.” She even remembered my name.

She said, "You’re Robert, right?'”

Jim said, “She remembered your name?”

“That surprised me, too. I asked how her place was going and she said okay. And then she asked if I wanted to see it. So I went to the loft and ended up helping her clean her windows on the outside. And she had used masking tape to show where she needed partitions built and I volunteered to build the partitions for her."

Gary said, "Partitions? You mean walls?"

"Yeah."

"You know how to do that?"

Robert said, "Yeah, built them when I was kid and do it on the job I have now."

Jim said, "Did you and her do anything?"

He nodded and solemnly said, "Yes we did." Then he paused for several seconds to see their expressions, and continued, "After we washed the windows, we went to lunch. That's it. She's a very nice person."

Gary said, "Yeah, a nice person with a heck of a body."

"Well, she's way out of my league, not to mention that she has a college professor boyfriend."

Gary said, "Well, that's too bad. Every guy's dream, an older woman."

Robert and Jim looked at Gary without saying anything and Gary continued, "Well, doesn't everybody think about an older woman?"

Robert said, "I guess."

Jim said, "Gary's already admitted that he still thinks about Mrs. Kirsten, and we've got a neighbor that always looks good to me. I wonder how many guys ever find that older woman."

Gary said, "Well, there's probably no good statistics on it because any guy that has the opportunity sure the heck's not gonna say anything about it." He looked Robert in the eyes and continued, "Right, Robert?"

Robert thought for a second, "I don't know, seems like guys would be bragging about something like that."

Gary doubtfully said, "Well, some might. But I don't think you would."

Jim said, "Another beer?"

They went back to the car and Robert and Gary took their guard positions while Jim poured three more beers.

Robert said, "Thanks Jim." They all put their cups together for a toast.

Jim said, "To good buddies and great diving. Now, that's the last of the beer so sip it slowly." They returned to the beach and sat back down.

Gary said, "So, you gonna build the walls?"

"I don't think so. With her boyfriend thing she has a busy life. I don't want to mess with lives that are working fine."

Alexia Calls

Alexia said, "Robert, now listen carefully to what I have to say. I feel terrible about the walls. It wasn't that I didn't want you to do the job, it's just that I wanted to be there and work with you." She started sobbing and continued, "I'm sorry, but when we did the windows together, it was, well, it was the best day that I've had in months. It was fun working with you. And I know that you could do the job yourself, but I wanted to be there and work with you. I didn't get a chance or I didn't know how to explain that to you before." She sniffs and is obviously very emotional and upset.

Robert said, "Don't cry. It'll be okay. I enjoyed working with you too. If you still want to go ahead with ordering the lumber, I can start next Saturday. But you have to promise that it won't interfere with you and boyfriend."

She sniffed and said, "Okay. Thank you."

Robert said, "I'll see you Saturday."

She sniffled again and said, “My new ocean view is quite incredible. Thank you.”

“You’re welcome.”

On Thursday Alexia called Robert and told him that the materials had been delivered and they even carried everything up to the loft.

Robert said, “Great. That'll speed things up.”

She said, “I love the smell of that new wood.”

“I know what you mean.”

She said, “I’ll leave the key above the door so come on in whatever time you get here on Saturday.”

“I’ll be there by eight, but don’t think you have to be there right away.”

“Thank you Robert. See you Saturday.”

Robert had settled down and almost accepted the fact that she had a boyfriend. He knew that nothing was going to happen between them anyway. He jumped himself up a notch too many and had get back into his own league. But Gary was right about the older woman fantasy. At the time he didn't realize it, but he was certain that his older woman fantasy started with Mrs. Randall, his piano teacher. And his more recent older woman experience happened in Santa Barbara. That was something that he would never get out of his mind and always wonder about. Mrs. Randall was more like a very pleasant experience and not really sexual like, but for some reason he kept the memory of her alive. Whereas the woman in Santa Barbara, well, she was very close to becoming his first valid sexual experience. Well, maybe not very close. But still, it was a pleasant experience, despite how it ended. He knew he had to stop thinking about this stuff so he tried to concentrate on Alexia’s project rather than her beauty, her body, her scent, and the fact that he just enjoyed being close to her. Actually, the only thing he didn't like about her was that she had a boyfriend. Hey, snap out of it. Concentrate on her project.

Robert got his tools together, making sure he had two hammers and several putty knives so that Alexia could get involved with the job. The week seemed to drag by for he was anxious to get started on the project. Saturday morning he pulled alongside the curb as close to Alexia's cannery as he could get because he had to carry the tools up to the loft. He noticed that Alexia's truck was parked along the curb nearby, which didn't surprise him because her boyfriend probably picked her up. He loaded his arms with the circular saw, drill and all of the tools that he could carry in one trip, climbed the stairs to the loft, and set the tools on the landing. He reached up on the ledge above the door and was relieved that the key was there as she said it would be. He returned to the car and picked up the rest of the tools and carried them up. As he was fumbling with getting the key in the lock, he had his hand on the doorknob and found that door was already unlocked. He shook his head thinking that he had already unlocked the door and didn't even remember. He nervously opened the door and the aroma of bacon seeped out. As he started bringing his tools into the loft, Alexia came out of the bathroom wearing her robe and looked like she hadn't been up very long. Not that she looked bad. Oh, no she looked really good, but he was embarrassed and thinking that he was too early.

"Good morning Robert. I heard coming up so I unlocked the door."

"Oh, I'm too early. Look, I'll go down by the ocean for a while." He didn't even look across the room to her bed because he assumed that her boyfriend was still there even though he hadn't seen his car. But maybe he was drunk and they took a cab or he parked in what he considered a better part of town.

She said, "No, come on in. Have a seat at the table." Hidden among the strong bacon aroma, was also the aroma of brewing coffee. She said, "Coffee?"

He nodded and she poured coffee into a very large mug. She said, "Some of the dishes were my grandfather's. Can you imagine that he and his friends were drinking out of these same mugs?"

He said, "You know, I'm not a very good student but you have a way of making history interesting."

She said, “Well, history is interesting. I think my grandfather was a good teacher.”

As Robert walked to the table he took a quick glance at her unmade bed and saw that it was empty. Maybe the boyfriend was in the bathroom. He watched Alexia put a plate of cooked bacon in the oven and she was cooking something on the stove top.

She said, "You like pancakes?”

He said, “Sure.”

She brought over a small pitcher of heated syrup and butter, and then carried over two plates, each containing a large pancake, and sat down. She sensed his anxiety and said, “I canceled my date last night. I really didn’t feel like going.”

Neither said much as they ate and when they were finished each picked up their plates and silverware and carried them to the kitchen.

"I’m gonna take a quick shower and get into my work clothes. You mentioned needing a ladder. There are several down stairs in the cannery. We can go down there when I get dressed and pick the one that you need."

Robert poured himself another cup of coffee and took a sip as he stood by the sink, and then started washing the dishes as he listened to the shower running. When Alexia came out she saw that all of the dishes had been washed.

She said, “Thank you. But you didn’t have to do that.”

He shrugged as though it was nothing and said, “That was a great breakfast.”

She smiled and said, “Thanks.”

As he followed her down the stairs into the cannery she said, “In the early thirties up until the late fifties this place employed nearly a hundred people, mostly women of several different backgrounds and nationalities. And look at it now. It’s like a museum that hasn’t been touched since the workers left." They brushed arms a few times as they walked together toward the far end of the cannery.

Alexia said, "I think I saw the ladders in a storeroom in that far corner. I don't come down here very often because it's a little spooky."

There were almost a half dozen ladders of different sizes in the storeroom and Robert also noticed quite a few tools like socket sets and large wrenches that must have been used to work on the cannery equipment. Robert picked the two shortest ladders and they each carried one to the loft.

Alexia held the tape measure as Robert took measurements for the partition that would separate the two bedrooms and butt up against the existing outside wall. He used the circular saw to cut the top plate and sole plate for the partition, then cut the studs and laid them all out on the floor to be nailed together. They attached the studs to the top plate and sole plate by drilling pilot holes to prevent splitting the wood and nailed them together. Then he cut another top plate that would be nailed to the ceiling for attaching the partition. He had Alexia get on the ladder and hold one end of the top plate against the ceiling as he held the other end. He drilled and nailed his end and then went over to Alexia's ladder and climbed up behind her trying not to get too close, but had to be close enough to reach around her shoulder and hold her end in place. Then he handed her the drill and said, "Make sure your end is on the line, and then drill the hole." She drilled it and he took the drill from her and handed her the hammer and a nail. With the predrilled hole, the nail went in easily. She looked down at Robert who was still standing on the second rung of the ladder and smiled.

He said, "Good job."

They stood the partition up and placed it under the top plate. Alexia held the partition while he used his level to plumb it, and then drew a line along the sole plate. As Alexia held the partition in place he drilled and nailed each end. Then he had Alexia drill and nail along the length of the sole plate and then drill and nail the top plate to the ceiling. Alexia finished nailing and smiled. Then she walked to the kitchen and admired the partition. They built and installed the second partition and then the front partition, which required adding a header and framing for the door frame. By noon they had one bedroom completely framed. Then Robert added the hinges and tested the door fit. Alexia must have opened and closed that door about six or seven times and smiled each time.

She said, "I guess there really is a Saco, Montana." Robert smiled. It was about noon, and Alexia made some tuna sandwiches and opened a bag of potato chips. She said, "You drink milk?"

"Yeah, I like milk."

They sat at the table so they both could see the new room. After lunch they framed the second bedroom and it was finished by four o'clock.

"So, the next step is to put up those the big panels, huh?"

"The drywall."

She said, "Oh right."

He said, "Before we install the drywall we have do the electrical."

She said, "Electrical? Oh, my gosh I forgot about that. I guess we do need some places to plug in lamps and clocks. I'll have to find an electrician. Aren't they the ones that do that stuff?"

"Yeah, but I can do it."

She said, "What do you mean, you can do it? Electricity is dangerous. You'll get shocked or electrocuted." Robert smiled as Alexia continued preaching, "No, this time I forbid you to risk your life. You got lucky with the window washing thing. But I won't let you get electrocuted." She was starting to get emotional and continued, "I don't want anything to happen to you. I'll get an electrical guy."

He quietly said, "Don't make tell you another Montana story."

"What do you mean?"

Robert said, "After the fire, we had moved back to Glasgow and my dad started another small automotive shop in an old building in an alley near downtown."

"What do you mean after the fire?"

"That's another story."

Alexia said, "I'd better start writing these other stories down."

"Well, Alexia, it seems that I'm telling all the stories around here. I'm gonna start expecting some from you."

She laughed and said, "No, I do the Monterey history, remember. You'd find my stories quite boring."

Robert looked into her eyes and seriously said, "I don't think so."

She said, "What about this Glasgow place after the fire that you aren't going to talk about yet?"

"Well, okay. If you remember, at that time most of the Christmas lights used those very large high-wattage bulbs that got hot enough to set Christmas trees on fire or give you a bad burn. Of course the large bulbs couldn't start any fires if they were outside in Montana in the wintertime when it was freezing cold, but they did use a lot of electricity and were large and cumbersome. Well, my Dad sometimes repaired seismograph trucks in his shop."

Alexia, looking puzzled said, "Seismograph trucks?"

"Oh, they're trucks used for gas and oil exploration. These trucks carry what my brothers and I called dynamite wire that is used to set off small charges to locate the gas and oil deposits. My dad bought a five hundred foot roll of this wire and got this idea of using the wire and the small six-volt automotive bulbs to make strings of miniature Christmas lights."

She said, "Oh, wow. He made his own Christmas lights?"

"Well, he started soldering the small bulbs onto the wire making sure we were watching and after he had soldered about four bulbs in place, he had us boys take over the soldering job. So this was our introduction to working with electricity. If you use six-volt bulbs and put twenty of these bulbs in series, then each bulb will get six of the one hundred twenty volts from an electrical outlet."

She, nodded and said, "Now, that's a practical math lesson."

He continued, "But to decorate a yard you need more than one string of twenty lights. So we made over ten strings of lights and strung them outside our house and had the first miniature lights in Montana or so we thought. But, if one of the strings of light went out we had to go out in the cold weather and use an ohmmeter on each of the bulbs in the string to find the bad bulb. And once we found it we had to try to keep the soldering gun hot enough to replace the bad bulb. So, that was our introduction to working with electricity."

Alexia said, "That's amazing. You know, I'm starting to see why you are like you are."

Robert smiled and said, "You mean an egghead?"

She laughed and said, "Yeah." And then continued, "No, I mean, I don't what I mean, but I'll figure that out and get back to you."

Robert laughed and said, "It's getting kind of late. Don't you have a date tonight?"

She said, "I don't really want to go."

He said, "No, you should go. You already cancelled out once."

She said, "Well, you have to promise you won't hook up any electricity until I'm here with you."

He nodded and said, "I'll get started with the electrical boxes and run the wire. I brought some boxes and wire with me."

She said, "You going to use dynamite wire?"

He laughed and said, "No, I'm a little bit beyond dynamite wire. I have a roll of the correct wire and I won't be working on hot circuits."

She said, “What do you mean hot circuits?”

He said, “A circuit that has the electricity turned on.”

She said, “Well, okay, but save some electrical work for me. Robert, I guess I have to take a shower and get dressed. Now, don’t think you have to go, but I’ll be dressing in my new bedroom. And those partitions, well you can see right through them.”

Robert, initially embarrassed, managed to teasingly say, “I won’t look.”

She gave a loud huff, and said, “Well now, that would be a hell of an insult.”

He laughed and went to the stack of drywall, separated a set of two sheets, carried one over and set it up against the partition and then carried another. She got the idea and started helping him partition off enough of her room to have some privacy.

She walked to him, gave him a hug and said, “You're so creative.”

He heard the shower running as he started drilling holes in the studs of the second bedroom to run the wiring for the electrical boxes. He had the boxes installed when he heard the shower turn off and then about five minutes later a robed person with a towel over her head rushed by and said, “Hi.” He managed a glance at her calves as she shut the door. Robert seemed to think she took her time shutting the door, which may have been wishful thinking or maybe not. She wasn’t beyond a little teasing.

He had the switch and outlet boxes installed and started the wiring run when he heard the bedroom door open, and a different person stepped out of the room. He looked at her, well, maybe more like a stare, and she smiled. He said, “Wow, you look nice.”

She said, “Thanks. But I wish I didn’t have to go. I’d rather be in my jeans working with you.” She raised her eyebrows and continued, “You coming tomorrow?”

He said, “Yeah, if you want me to. I can finish the electrical and we can start on the drywall.”

Blaine Arrives

She laid a dry towel on the board between two sawhorses sat down and watched him wire the boxes. Then there was a knock at the door. She went to answer it. Robert heard a voice and saw a tall thin guy with glasses, wearing a suit, who he assumed was her boyfriend. He seemed to be more handsome than Robert wanted him to be. He would have preferred a brainier look, maybe more of a goofy looking guy.

Alexia said, "Robert, this is my friend Blaine." Robert, standing behind the newly framed partition, waved and Blaine returned a stiff, superior nod.

Blaine said, “Alexandria, my goodness, what have you done in here? It looks like a wall of sorts.”

When Robert heard Blaine talk, cars came to mind. He thought to himself, you can have the best looking car in the world but if the engine doesn’t sound right, what good is it. Appearance will not carry a person or a car very far. Now, Robert was a little more at ease, because this Blaine guy’s crummy personality and rudeness seemed to override any handsomeness that he might have.

Blaine stepped in further, apparently further than he had ever been before, and as he looks at the drywall they temporarily placed for privacy, snickered and said in a seemingly fake British like voice, “It looks rather amateurish don’t you think?” Robert was holding the claw hammer as he peered through the studs. Blaine glared at Robert and in a loud enough voice to ensure Robert could hear, “Alexandria, so, this is your master carpenter. Well, I could believe masturbator, for his work gives one the impression that he is merely a boy pretending to be a carpenter and probably wanted to be a fireman just last week. And that must have been, well still is I must assume, his relic parked in the street. I parked some distance away to ensure the shoddiness of it doesn't rub off on my Porsche."

Robert was trying to determine whether to use the circular saw, an inch-and-a quarter boring bit in the drill, or go in with the hammer. The hammer would be quite effective in the hands of a very pissed off person, just a little messier. Yet, a very angry person with fast fist to the nose would more than likely send this guy running off to his wealthy mommy. But, he merely glared at Blaine and wondered how Alexia could stand to be around this asshole. At least being an asshole overrode any kind of attraction that he had. But he couldn't be angry at Alexia. He didn't want to make her life difficult. Maybe Blaine turned into a nice guy when they were by themselves. Or maybe this is how overly educated people with inherited money act. He respected and trusted her and assumed that she was handling the situation the way she thought best. Robert finally started thinking that Blaine would give Chester, the Glasgow, Montana pool manager, a little time off, but it wouldn't change his lifetime goal of pissing on Chester's grave. No, his life was only made more complex, for he now had two life time goals. That's all he needed, a more complex life. When does the complexity stop? Now, two graves to piss on.

Alexia approached Robert and kissed him on the cheek. God she smells good, he thought. That seeming simple kiss had neutralized some of the best anger that he had built up in a long time and now it was gone. Well, the anger was gone, but he was determined to hang onto the hatred for this guy with the stupid name. Alexia whispered, "I'm sorry, I think he's jealous. Please don't work too late. I want you to have a safe trip home. I'll see you tomorrow?" Robert just nodded. Now he felt like a boy pretending to be a carpenter, but was still thinking of the kiss on the cheek. He wondered if asshole had seen that. As she and Blaine started out the door, she handed Robert the spare key that had been above the doorway that morning, squeezed his hand, and said, "Hang on to this."

That kiss, and now the key made Robert feel so superior to that guy. He had his own key to her loft. He wondered how a mere boy could make a wealthy college professor with doctorate in philosophy jealous. He started feeling better about the situation. Then suddenly, he wondered something. He wondered if Alexia had left any lipstick on his cheek. He went into the bathroom and looked in the mirror. He nodded and smiled. Sure, he'd had lipstick on his face before, but this was a real woman's lipstick. He was starting to feel good. And now he was by himself and that was okay too because it was like he had own apartment for the night. And he figured that she was too nice, too pretty, and too smart to be with this Blaine guy very long.

He had to gain access to an electrical supply for the new circuits in the bedrooms. He cut a small hole up through the top plate of the new partition and ceiling and pushed his new electrical line through the hole into the attic area. He located an access to the attic in a kitchen closet and crawled up into the attic and was amazed how large it was. He visualized there could be another room up here with a great view. He found the group of electrical lines that went down to the switchbox below and was able to push his new line down to the switchbox. He crawled out of the attic, retrieved his line, shut the main power switch off and connected the line to a switch. After turning the main power switch on, he located a lamp and set it on the small table next to Alexia's bed, plugged it into a newly installed outlet, and turned the lamp on. He smiled when he thought about Alexia coming home and seeing the lamp on.

He moved the drywall that they had propped up temporarily to make Alexia's bedroom, stacked it with the other sheets and then took the scrap wood down to the cannery. After sweeping the entire loft, he went to his car, opened the trunk, and moved his wetsuit aside, exposing a small cooler. He opened the cooler and removed three of the six beers that were cooling on ice. But then he hesitated, put one beer back and closed the cooler and the trunk. He walked up the stairs to the loft with the two beers in one hand. Whenever he carried something like this he thought of the evenings he spent working far beyond midnight as a pin setter in the Glasgow bowling alley where he could pick up two pins with one hand. Typically the bowling alley stayed open until the last bowler left, and it was not uncommon for that bowler to be Harry Akin, a farmer, who was nearly seven feet tall, and so strong that the pin setter moved into another lane when his ball left his hand. When Harry's ball hit those pins, they would not merely fall over as with an average bowler, they would fly up onto the bench where the pin setter sat. As he thought about Harry Akin, he wondered if Harry's goal was to knock out a pin setter, and maybe he had on occasion. Most of the pin setters felt that Harry could easily have bowled overhand, if management had let him.

With the beers in one hand, he put the other hand in his pocket and felt the key that Alexia had given him. He didn't need the key because the door was still unlocked. He just wanted to feel it. He put the two beers in the freezer compartment of her refrigerator and found a tall glass in the cupboard. He looked around and made sure that everything was in its place and the tools and all of the materials were neatly stacked. When Alexia returned from her date, he wanted her to walk into the loft that now had the appearance of becoming a really nice place. Then he went to the freezer and pulled out a beer and poured the entire can into the glass, tipping it slightly to avoid too much foam. Using his two hands, he compressed the steel can with a twisting motion, a talent that had taken quite a long time to perfect. And he thought to himself, could jackass do that? Could that fake British snob smash a steel can with his bare hands? Does jackass have a key to her loft? No, he knew she wouldn't give someone like that Blaine guy a key. Then he turned off the lights and sat down at the table and watched the sunset through the now sparkly windows that he and Alexia had cleaned. Could Blaine have done that? Could jackass have risked his life sitting on that windowsill? Robert thought, hell, that jackass couldn't have even used the Phillip's head screwdriver. Then he laughed to himself. Then he laughed at himself. This project was good for him. The beer went down fast and he opened the second can and after pouring, performed the miraculous can smashing trick one more time, and sipped his second beer while taking in the ocean air and sort of wished he'd brought up the third beer.

Finishing the Partitions

The radio was playing a Bobby Darin song, "Dreaming I'm always dreaming, someday you'll be mine." It wasn't surprising that at seven o'clock Sunday morning the traffic was light. Even though he didn't get to bed until eleven o'clock, he woke up early. He planned to walk out on the wharf to kill some time, for he didn't want to wake up Alexia if she was there or perhaps he didn't want to know if she wasn't. He parked near the entrance to the wharf and walked toward the end. Mornings are an interesting time because trucks are delivering fresh fish and vegetables to the restaurants and the restaurant employees are preparing their shops for the day. He looked inside a bar that had the door open and reeked of cigarette smoke and stale beer as a young guy was picking up glasses and bottles and emptying ashtrays from tables. By the time Robert reached the end of the wharf, it was a quarter to eight so he turned around and slowly walked back to his car and drove to her cannery. He stood at entrance to the loft for a while before tapping lightly, and was very surprised when the door opened, and Alexia stood there in her working jeans, with the sweet scent of, just stepping out of the shower, radiating from her body.

She smiled and said, “Good morning, Robert. Have you eaten?”

Robert said, “I had some cereal.”

She said, “Well, I'm going to cook some eggs. Pour yourself some coffee”

He casually walked behind her, picked up a coffee mug from the counter, feeling almost like he lived here, poured a cup of coffee, sat at the table and watched her cook. She brought two plates of eggs and a plate of buttered toast over and sat down with him and they ate. She smiled and said, “This place looked so nice when I came in last night. I must have sat in that chair and looked at it for half hour. So, we gonna hang drywall today?” Robert nodded and smiled.

As he was carrying a sheet of drywall into the spare bedroom he said, “We'll start in the spare bedroom and once the seams are taped we can move your bedroom furniture into that room. These sheets are installed across the studs like this rather than up and down.” The partition they started with had an electrical outlet box that he had installed. He opened the spackle container and used his finger to dab spackle around the lip of the box.

Alexia said, “What's that for?”

He said, "You'll see in a minute." He put the first sheet up against the partition making sure to press it tightly against the lip of the outlet box. Then when he pulled the sheet away from the partition, the outline of the outlet box was imprinted on the drywall.

Alexia said, “Quite clever.”

He smiled and handed her the keyhole saw to cut out a section for the outlet box. Alexia helped him position the drywall so the outlet box was sticking through. He had her hold the drywall while he put a couple nails along the top to hold it in place.

He said, “Now grab a hammer and some of those nails. About every twelve inches nail the drywall to the studs.”

She started pounding her first nail and said, "Shit." The nail had bent.

He laughed and grabbed a short piece of scrap two-by-four, stood close to her and guided her hand and said, “Put the claw of your hammer here and use this of wood block between the drywall and the hammer and pull the nail out. This is so you won't tear the drywall and it also makes it easier to pull the nail.” She gently pulled on the hammer handle and the nail popped out.

She nodded and said, “Pretty neat.”

Then she picked up another nail and he said, “It's best to put the new nail in a different spot. Just put it close by.” She pounded the second nail in. He said, “The head of the nail has to be slightly below the surface of the drywall so we can cover it with the spackle.” He lightly hit her nail with his hammer driving the head into the drywall without tearing the surface and said, “Now feel the nail head with your finger. See how it dimples in? When we spackle over the nail head the dimple will be filled in.” She took another nail and pounded it in and then tapped the head until it until it was almost below the surface. She used her finger and felt that it was still sticking out a little so she hit it again.

She said, “How's that?"

He said, “It looks good. You're getting it”

They finished nailing the bottom sheet of drywall in place and continued around the room and until all four partitions had the bottom sheet in place. Then Robert measured the area above the bottom sheet and discovered they had to take one inch off the top sheet. He showed Alexia how to score the drywall with the knife and then snap the drywall along the scored line and cut off the unwanted piece with the knife. Then they put the top sheet in place and Alexia held the sheet while Robert pulled the ladder over and put two nails in the top to hold it up. They nailed the bottom portion of the sheet as high as they could reach and Robert spread out the sawhorses and placed a board across them for a place to stand. They both got up on the board and started nailing the top sheet, working toward each other. Soon they were standing together and she turned, smiled and said, “My arm is starting to ache. But it feels good.”

He said, “Well we can give it a rest while we're doing the seams and the nail heads.” Robert laid out a drop cloth that covered entire floor of the room. Then he mixed up a thin mixture of spackle in a container and then had another container of water. He cut the first piece of tape, soaked it in the water and used his fingers to remove the excess water. Then he put the tape into the spackle mixture and as he pulled it out, he removed the excess spackle from the tape. He put the tape on the first seam and pulled a wide putty knife down over the seam to remove the excess spackle and press the tape against the drywall.

Alexia watched him. He said, “You want to try one?”

She said, “Sure.”

He said, “The spackle will take the moisture out of your hands. Do you have rubber gloves?” She went into the kitchen and returned wearing yellow rubber gloves. She cut the proper length for a seam, soaked it in the water and then into the spackle mixture. He helped her apply the tape to a seam, and she pulled the putty knife down along the seam. She smiled. They finished taping the room. And then they started spackling the nail heads.

He said, “If you come across any nail heads that are still sticking out give them another tap with the hammer.” She seemed to be having a good time covering the nail holes and they finished them up quickly, and then he said, “The spackle will shrink when it dries, so each nail hole might have to be re-coated. This is something that you can do during the week if you have time.” They picked up the drop cloth, swept the room, and then stood close together in the doorway admiring their work.

She put her arm around him, looked at him and said, "It’s a real room.” Robert smiled and nodded. She smiled and said, “Thank you. You ready for some lunch?”

Robert said, “There’s a hamburger place up on the hill. Let’s walk up there and I’ll buy you a burger.”

She nodded said, “Sounds good. You know you're a mess.” She reached up with her hand and removed a large spatter of spackle from his forehead. He took a deep breath as she stood close to him.

He said, “Yeah, I know. Guess I should wash my face before we go.”

After lunch they moved the furniture out of her bedroom and installed the drywall, taped it and applied the first coat over the nail heads. Then they moved the furniture back into her room. It was about five o’clock when they finished and then he temporarily put both of the bedroom doors on.

Robert said, “If all of the seams look okay after they dry I may be able to put the final texture coat on next weekend if you're going to be available."

She nodded and said, “I can hardly wait. Oh, and when you come next Saturday, bring an extra pair of jeans and a sweater and I’ll take you to dinner.”

“That sounds good, but you don’t have to do that.”

“I want to.”

He said, “You might as well take your key back.”

"Why don't you hang to it for a while?" She gave him a hug and kissed him on the cheek.

His week went rather slowly, but finally Saturday morning arrived and he was on his way to Monterey. The radio was playing a Don Gibson song,

"Everybody's going out and having fun. I'm just a fool for staying home and having none. I can't get over how she set me free oh lonesome me."

Uninvited Visit

Alexia woke early to the sun shining into her room. She went into the kitchen and put on a pot of coffee and was smiling as she entered the shower, staying much longer than she usually did. She put on fresh jeans and tried on several different blouses before selecting one and then went to the kitchen and cooked bacon while preparing pancake batter. As she sipped coffee, a tap on the door put a smile on her face. She excitedly opens the door, and he said, "I haven't seen a smile like that from you for a while." Then with even more emphasis, "A long while."

Her smile quickly changed to a glare, "What are you doing here?"

"I worried about you and wondered if you were okay and just happened to be in the neighborhood." He looked around the room and saw that the rooms were more complete and both bedroom doors were shut. He continued in his irritating snobbish voice, "Have company?"

"It's not really any of your business, is it?"

"Well, I miss you, that's all. I think we could put all of this preposterousness behind us. I came to apologize to you and to the boy."

"That's enough. You have to go now."

Blaine took a deep breath and said, "That coffee aroma is delightfully homey."

As Robert approaches her cannery, an acute ache strikes his gut and a feeling of deception runs through his mind, for Blaine's car is parked at the curb. He slows down but keeps driving and wishing he had his old life back. It was too painful for him to like someone too much. He should have stuck with Lynnette, and started thinking maybe he could work things out with her. Yeah, he could have handled that better. He heads toward the entrance to the Monterey Highway, but at the last minute turns off before heading toward Salinas, and ends up at the wharf. He sat in the car for a while listening to the radio and then got out and walked down to the end of the wharf and watched the sea lions, wondering if they had problems like he was having. In his old life, the ocean always made him feel good. But now that he had a taste of being with somebody that he liked, he felt empty. It was as though he now needed someone to appreciate life with him in order for him to appreciate life. And that feeling was too foreign and far too complex. Having to rely on somebody else was like needing a crutch and a severe jolt to his independence. As he walked back toward his car, he started thinking a little more rationally. Alexia didn't hide the fact that she has a boyfriend. What is she supposed to do, give it all up for him? He had agreed to do a job for her and that is what he had to do. He couldn't blame her. Then he smiled to himself, because he was glad that her boyfriend was an asshole. But those thoughts were short lived, for he knew he was being selfish. She doesn't deserve him thinking that way. Not only that, she's just a good friend. A good friend that he likes being with. That's what she is, a good friend in a sister way. Well, maybe not a like a sister. Maybe more like a fantasy or an actress that you really like but know you will never be romantically involved with, except in your mind. He felt that way about that actress, what's her name, oh yeah, Audrey Hepburn. Alexia wasn't his girl friend, she was just a friend and he was just her carpenter friend. And she was fun to be with.

Alexia looked at the clock. It was nine and she worried that Robert had seen Blaine's car parked outside or he had been in an accident. She didn't even know if he made it home safely last night. She reluctantly had given Blaine a cup of coffee because he promised to leave when he finished. She sat across the table from him, impatiently tapping her finger and scowling, in hopes that he would get the message. Blaine had a hard time imagining that a person could not want him around. She wondered what his mother thought of him. Did she want him around? Then there was a knock on the door. She jumped up from the chair and hurried to the door.

Blaine said, “Well, there he is now. At least he didn’t spend the night unless you gave him some money earlier and sent him on an errand to pick up a paper or sweep the stoop.”

Alexia turned toward Blaine, giving him a disgusted look, opened the door and grabbed Robert’s hand, pulled him inside and gave him a long hug, and said, “I was so worried about you.”

Blaine said, “Oh, I'm so glad you stopped by. Alexia said that I owe you an apology. So, I apologize. Now, don’t take that lightly because it is something that I seldom have to do. But I do have respect for Alexia and her little friends. And as a side note, if you are having a problem getting dates with girls your own age, I can probably find something for you, for I am a professor at a distinguished college. And there a few girls that are not, well let’s say proper enough, for the level of most of our students. You know, like the ones on scholarships that have limited resources, probably much like yourself. They often come from that city down the road, huh, the lettuce place, Salinas, that has that rancid odor of celery when I scurry through on my way to the city.”

Robert stared at Blaine in amazement and disbelief that this idiot could ramble on with goofy jabber. Rather than anger, Robert was becoming amused because the babbling from this over-educated idiot was reminding him of a drunk on Market Street in Salinas that he and Carl had run across in their quest to buy beer. It was the way he rambled on. The only difference is that Robert respected the drunk on Market Street and called him sir, even though Carl said the drunk was not a sir. But Robert still called him sir out of respect for his age and what he may have before he hit bottom. This Blaine guy did not rate a sir.

Robert with a very interested, but perhaps sarcastic expression said, “Gee, Mr. Blaine. A girl my own age, that’d be real swell of you.”

Blaine glared at Robert for several seconds and said, “You know, you better get rid of that sarcasm if you want make something of yourself you uneducated little shit. And frankly, I’m little tired you hanging around my girl. I worry about somebody like you that happens be in the neighborhood of this slum ridden street and shows up at her doorstep like a lost puppy."

Robert hesitated, for he was having a difficult time holding back a couple of puppy barks. Alexia looked at Robert and knew exactly what he was thinking and smiled a little. But he held his barks and with a straight face, merely said, "It's been real swell talking with you Mr. Blaine, but I have to get to work." Robert turned, walked into the spare bedroom, shut the door and started randomly pounding as loudly as he could on a piece of scrap wood that was on the floor and the hammering was echoing throughout the loft. After about a minute or so he heard the front door shut.

Alexia opened the bedroom door and came in, shook her head and hugged him. He could feel her tears on his cheek, while she said, "I was so worried about you being late. I was afraid you wouldn't come if you saw his car. He showed up and I couldn't get rid of him. I'm so sorry."

Robert felt guilty about his previous thoughts and actions, and they continued hugging. He said, "It's okay, it's not your fault."

She said, "I guess I'm so used to being around people like him that I've become immune to the way they act. Then I'm around someone like you and I can see the contrast." She sniffed and went into the bathroom to rinse her face off and came out and gave sigh and said, "Get yourself some coffee and I'll start the pancakes. I redid all of the nail holes. Hope I didn't miss any."

They finished eating and while she was doing the dishes he looked over the tape and nail holes and everything looked smooth enough to go ahead with final texture. He said, "Alexia, you did a great job on the nail holes. Everything looks really good."

They moved the furniture out of both bedrooms into living room and laid down the drop cloth in her bedroom. He mixed up the spackle with a small amount fine sand to get the skipping effect that he wanted. He started texturing the ceiling and then moved to each new partition. When he was finished he carefully inspected the room, touched up a couple of areas, and moved the drop cloth into the spare bedroom. By four o'clock, he had finished texturing.

He said, "We might have to retexture the other walls in the loft if they don't match but I think they will be okay." He opened up the living room and bedroom windows to speed up the drying process and they moved the furniture back into the two bedrooms.

Alexia walked around to several different locations in the loft and said, "It looks amazing. Thanks, Robert. I feel like we need some champagne or something to celebrate with. I don't even have any wine."

Robert said, "I've got a couple beers in the car."

Alexia said, "You know, that sounds good."

Robert went to his car for the beer. He was surprised that she didn't say anything about him having beer considering his age. It must mean something that she doesn't consider him a kid that he thought he was. And he was amazed that there was still ice in the cooler so the four cans of beer were quite cold and he was glad that he only drank two last night. He pulled the four cans out and carried them to the loft.

Robert said, "Hope you like Coors."

She said, "That's fine with me." He walked to the cupboard and brought over two glasses and poured each of them a beer. She held her glass to his, and as they toasted they looked at each other and took a sip.

She said, "I don't mention this place to most of the people I work with. Maybe it's a matter of pride and lack of confidence. When I have a new project going, I usually don't tell many about it until I know how it's going to turn out. I guess that's so I don't have to worry about explaining failure except to myself. And it allows me to start impossible projects."

Robert said, "So what other impossible projects have you started?"

She laughed and said, "Well, I was one of those kids who always had a Cool Aid stand going in the summer and then I started a neighborhood newspaper. We featured the yard of the month and other valuable neighborhood information. Like who had a new baby and who moved in or out of the neighborhood. My projects escalated from there. In college I did lot of temporary work for people. Like housecleaning, typing, house sitting, and pet sitting and things like that. But I couldn't handle all of the jobs so I started a temporary agency using other students. But I was very careful whom I hired to keep the quality of work. So pretty soon I was so busy running the little business, it became my full time part time job. It could have become a full time business, but I wanted to finish school so I turned it over to a friend. She let it go downhill and it didn't last very long." She took a sip of beer and continued, "It's funny, I forgot about those things. I guess because nobody ever asked about it. And yet, when I think of it, they seem like a very important part of my life. I don't think Blaine even knows what state I came from. And you know why, because he doesn't care. He doesn't give a shit. He only cares about himself. In fact, in the upper level academic world it seems that everybody has to pretend and defend their importance. Their respect comes from diplomas and getting something published. The parties we go to are full of people talking about themselves. I guess that's why the last few days working with you have been so nice. I can be myself." She finished her beer.

Robert said, "Another?" She nodded and he opened two more.

She continued, "Right now, I'm thinking that the Cool Aid stands were as important as any degrees that I have. My grandfather always said to have a plan for the future but make the most each day because some of the things that you do each day, may not seem important at the time, but later in life they might have more value than you realize. That's why you should make the most of each day."

"So what about you, Robert?"

"I already used up most my stories. I grew up in a couple of different small towns in Northeastern Montana. My brother and I did a lot of small jobs like yard work and putting up storm windows in the fall and taking them down in the spring. My family didn't have storm windows. We taped plastic sheeting to the outside of the windows in the two very small bedrooms. The windows would still accumulate about a quarter-inch of frost on the inside during most of the winter. We used to write stuff on the frosty windows or put our handprints in the frost. It was kind of like having a frozen chalkboard. We did have real jobs, too. In Saco there were two grocery stores. My younger brother delivered groceries for one of the grocery stores and I delivered groceries for the other." Then he smiled, and continued, "Oh, and we were also in the theatre business"

Alexia smiled and said, "The theatre business?"

Robert laughed and said, "Yeah, we cleaned the Saco theatre. He and I had every kid job in town."

She said, "Where were the other kids?"

Robert said, "Well, it was farming and ranching community so a lot of the kids lived on their farms. Yet, there were at least ten other kids in town that could have done these jobs. I don't know how we got all of the jobs. And when we weren't doing our grocery and theatre jobs we helped clean our dad's hardware store and garage and did inventories of hardware and parts and even put together harvesters. When the harvesters come on the train from the factory, there are certain parts that have to be installed. It was fun putting on the wooden slats that push the grain into the steel cutters where the wheat is cut."

She said, "I don't know how you guys found the time."

"Well, there was no television."

She nodded and said, "Yeah, that could free up a lot of time. You know, as a matter of fact, I don't have a television. I almost forgot about that. Oh, did you remember that I'm taking you to dinner tonight? I have reservations at Antonio's at the end of the wharf. We should get ready. I'm going to take a shower. Why don't you use the second bedroom to change clothes and take a shower in the other bath?"

Dinner with Alexia

Alexia had eaten in Antonio's many times as young girl with her grandfather and recently by herself, so she knew Antonio, the owner, quite well and he always treated her very special, as he had her grandfather. When Robert and Alexia entered, Antonio greeted her with a kiss and hug. She introduced Robert as her friend.

Antonio said, “Well, any friend of Alexia’s is especially welcome here.” He escorted the two of them to a small table in the back that overlooked the bay. Antonio continued, “How would you two like a nice bottle of wine that’s on me?” Robert worried that Antonio might check his ID, but he didn't seem concerned about it.

They sat down and Antonio poured their first glass of wine and left the bottle. Alexia picked up her glass and said, “Here’s to the loft that you have become big part of." They put their glasses together and each took a sip. Alexia continued, "I was getting quite depressed about the project to a point where I thought I’d taken on too much. Thanks to you, Robert, I am feeling very good about it now. Not only have I learned a lot from you about building partitions, I’m also having fun working with you.”

Robert said, “I think I needed this project. It’s been a while since I have had a sense of accomplishment. It seems like working with you is just something that was meant to be, like destiny.”

She said, “Destiny, huh. That’s interesting.”

He said, “Yeah, It sounds weird, huh?”

She shook her head and said, “No, no, it doesn’t.”

He continued, “Well, you know, a lot of seemingly unplanned things had to take place for my family, who spent a lifetime in Montana, to move to California. Not only that, my brother and I had been practicing diving since we were very young. Practicing diving in Montana where nobody dives. It seemed like something was pushing us to get ready for being here. This destiny idea hit me when I was sitting on my air mattress out in the Cove and looked down into water. I felt everything that has happened to our family was so my brother and I could be here.”

Alexia, intriguingly, “Funny you mentioned that. I mean destiny. I’ve thought about that when it came to me moving out here. You don’t know this, but I was supposed to get married a year ago. Been going with him for quite a while and it just seemed to be something that everybody, including my fiancé assumed.”

He said, “But you didn’t?”

She shook her head and smiled, and said, “I don’t know. I guess maybe I wasn’t convinced.” She thought for a while and continued, “When I received the news about inheriting the cannery, it was like someone had sent me an escape mechanism, a one way ticket to Monterey. I asked him if he would come with me, and obviously he didn’t. Maybe marriage wasn’t part of what was meant to be. Like you said, It’s almost like I was suppose to live out here. I’ve never mentioned or talked to anybody about this before. Not every person could go along with the idea because it’s so mystifying.”

He said, “That’s true. I’ve never talked about this. Not even to my family.”

She said, “If you look at our situation, you have two individuals, each with different backgrounds, who came a couple thousand miles from different places, end up meeting and working together. Is it all by chance? It seems like you could easily believe that it’s not. If I told this to the people that know I live on Cannery Row, it would further enhance their belief that I’m nuts.”

Robert nodded and laughed, "Well, it seems like you're taking over where Doc Ricketts left off. Maybe that’s all part of the overall plan. And it's best that others don't discover it, for they’ll all want to do it. I think you’re ahead of your time.”

Alexia smiled “Maybe so. I wish my grandfather was around to join this conversation. I think it’s something he would have been interested in.”

Robert said, “He must have been quite a guy.”

She nodded and smiled, “Yeah, he was. Maybe all the summers I spent out here with him were all part of the plan.”

He said very seriously, “You know, I’m starting to think that you might be right. I mean why not? When you think of the complexity of a person or just about any living thing, why would it be completely out of line to think that your life could possibly be laid out for you?”

She nodded and said, “I can’t think of a reason.”

“You know Alexia, I like talking with you.”

She smiled, “Thank you. That’s nicest complement I’ve heard since I’ve been out here.”

They both ordered Abalone and drank another of glass of wine. During the meal they finished off the bottle and Antonio came by and asked if they wanted another bottle. Alexia thanked him but said they had to be able to walk home. Antonio smiled and seemed to have that look in his eye, that they were a couple. Well, that’s what Robert was thinking, anyway. Antonio winked and said, "Well you two have nice evening. And don't think about trying to pay for the meal. If you do, Leroy over there will put one of you under each arm and carry you out like light luggage.”

As they walked toward the cannery, Alexia said she wanted to pick up another bottle of wine so they went up to Lighthouse Avenue to a small liquor store, got the wine and continued to the cannery. As they climbed the stairs to the loft, Robert stayed close behind her because he was afraid she might fall. Once they reached the landing at the top of the stairs, she struggled to get the key into the lock and backed into him. While still lingering against him, she turned her head, and slurred, “Sorry.” Once inside, Alexia said, “We’ve both had plenty to drink, so I don’t think it is a good idea for you to drive home. I think you should stay in our new guest bedroom tonight.”

“I’ll be fine in half hour.”

“Well, I was thinking about opening this other bottle of wine and christening the room.”

“Sounds like you've already made up your mind."

Alexia, clinched her jaw, nodded and said, “Yep.” She handed him the bottle and continued, “There’s an opener in the top drawer.”

He opened the bottle and poured each of them a glass and they toasted the room as they sat on the couch. He said, "I've been wondering about something."

"Something about me?"

"Sort of."

She nodded, slurred a bit and slowly said, "Well then, maybe I can be of assistance."

He laughed and said, "When the three of us met you the first time, did you remember all of our names?"

She thought for a second and said, "No, no, I did not."

"Why did you remember mine?"

"I don't know. I guess you impressed me the most. You stood out."

"That's interesting, because I don't try to stand out."

She said, "Well, I think that's what's impressive about you. That's what I like about you."

He said, "You know, when I was in the fourth grade I was playing soccer during PE. I always worked hard in PE. But this one day my right side hurt really bad. But I didn't stop playing. It wasn't because I was brave or anything. I just didn't want to call attention to myself. So after school I went home and my Mom called the doctor. We walked four blocks down to the doctor's office. That evening I was in the hospital getting my appendices out. But you know what? I got a fuckin' C in PE that year."

She laughed a little and said, "A fuckin' C?"

He said, "Yeah, a fuckin' C. You would think that a PE teacher with twelve kids in the class could figure out who was producing and trying their best. I wish I could remember that teacher's name."

She curiously said, "Why?"

He took a sip of wine, nodded and said, "Well, I'd put him on my list."

Now she frowned and said, "Your list?"

Robert said, “Yeah, I’m keeping a list of the people whose graves I’m going to piss on and I’d forgotten about him.”

Alexia nodded, and with very a straight face said in an encouraging teacher’s voice, “What a wonderful idea, Robert.” And her straight face worked, for Robert burst into laughter and she couldn’t hold back any longer and started laughing along with him. When both stopped laughing, Alexia slurred, “Robert, I have tip for you.” She hesitated, nodded very seriously and continued, “Don’t ever mention that list to a shrink.” Robert laughed again.

Robert said, “I know I’m talking too much. It’s just coming out.”

Alexia put her warm hand on his arm and said, “No, this is nice. I like hearing you talk.”

He said, “You know, I strive for a simple life. I don’t like clutter and frills and stuff. When I bought my car, it had about two hundred pounds of extra stuff. It had vertical bumper guards on the front and rear bumpers, a sun device above the windshield, and fender skirts. I took it all off. A lot of guys my age are interested in having special hubcaps, mufflers and other extra stuff. I like being in the background.”

She said, “Well, it’s not working for you. When I first saw you with your two friends, it was you who stood out. I couldn’t help it. You know there seems to be something about you that radiates that you are a simple, honest person with no distracting frills”

He said, "That’s funny. I try not to be noticed but it makes me noticed, by trying not to be noticed, so I stand out.”

She laughed and said, “I’ll bet you couldn’t say that sentence again.”

He laughed and said, “Probably not. It Reminds me of this Bob Newhart show where Bob goes to a Farrell’s ice-cream shop with a group of people. He’s been there before and knew of the singing waiters and waitresses. He doesn't want fanfare, so he plays it safe and orders a single scoop of vanilla. He gets the single scoop and takes a single bite, and here they come. Six irritating waiters and waitresses, all decked out in their frilly uniforms, surround Bob and sing, “Single scupper party pooper, every party has a pooper.” Alexia laughed.

Robert said, “I know this guy who likes guys. We ran around together for a while in Salinas when he lived there.”

She very seriously nodded and said, "Oh, really, so, you two were real close?"

He laughed and said, "No, not like that. He is just a good friend. I just ran with him, I didn’t date him.” Alexia laughed. “Actually, the only experience I had with a guy was in high school history class. We were in a dark auditorium watching a history movie and this guy sitting next to me, who I’d known all year, started rubbing my thigh and asked me if it felt good. I didn’t know what to do and didn’t say anything but sort of moved my leg away from him and he left me alone.”

She said, “Did he ever approach you again?”

“No, no he didn’t. Anyway, this guy I ran around with in Salinas moved to Santa Barbara. So one weekend I went to visit him and the three other guys he was living with.”

She laughed and said, “Oh really. That sounds interesting."

Robert said, "Well they liked guys, but they just treated me like a friend. They lived in an apartment complex and were acquainted with two neighbors upstairs, who were very attractive women in their mid twenties. So these two women invited us to a party they were having. They had plenty of beer and wine. And I guess I had about three or four beers and I don’t know how it happened, but I found myself slow dancing with one of these women, but the apartment was really crowded so we weren’t moving very fast or very far. Anyway, here I am holding this woman as we danced to a Johnny Mathis record, and it was the first time that I had held a real woman. I mean somebody that felt more substantial than a girl my age. I guess someone that was more filled out and soft and adult like and I started wondering why she was dancing with me. I still thought of myself, and still do, as an older boy. I wondered when a guy is considered a man. My head was spinning and instead of enjoying her body against mine I was thinking these dumb thoughts. I didn’t know what I was doing or what she was doing. All I knew was that I didn't deserve to be dancing with this woman. But at the same time I liked it. I liked it a lot. Everything seemed so right for something nice to happen.”

Alexia looked into his eyes with a questioning look and said, "Was there any part of your body that wasn't thinking? I mean any part that wasn't over analyzing the situation?” Robert looked confused, as she continued, “What I mean is, was there any part of you that ignored your thoughts and responded to the moment?" She raised her eyebrows in that questioning fashion.

And finally, Robert had that, light just came on look, smiled and said, “Oh, yeah, I think that was happening, and it was at that point I decided I no longer liked girls.”

Alexia laughed and said, “Oh, really."

Robert laughed and said, "You know what I meant."

"Yeah, I think I know. But go on."

Robert got up from the sofa and picked up the wine bottle, filled their glasses, and took a sip of his.

“So what happened? That can’t be the end of the story?”

“You're waiting for the steamy part, huh?”

“Of course, doesn’t everyone?”

“Well, we were very close together and barely moving. I was oblivious to everything around me and seemed to just melt into this woman. But then, I felt someone grab my left shoulder and then someone else grabbed my right shoulder and started pulling me away from her, and one of them said, ‘We have to get you out of here.’ Before I knew it, I was unwillingly heading downstairs to their apartment. Apparently this woman had an ex-boyfriend who had come to make up, but first take care of this person dancing with his woman.”

“Oh, no, I bet you were disappointed.”

“You know, I was at the time, but I don’t know if I was ready for her. I don’t even know if she felt the same way. This way my ego is still in tack because I can imagine, or maybe fantasize how things would have been if her boyfriend hadn’t come.”

Alexia said, “When did this happen?”

He said, “About a year ago.”

He noticed Alexia’s glass was still half full. He took another sip of his and continued, "So, I guess you sort of remind me of the woman I was dancing with. I guess holding, I mean dancing with you would be same."

Alexia said, “Well, it would be interesting to find out if it would be the same, but we really can’t.”

Robert, devastated said, “Oh, God, I’m sorry. Oh, Jesus. I started talking too much because you are easy to talk with. I took advantage of you. It was stupid to tell the story. I guess that’s what separates the boys from the men.”

She put her index finger across his lips and continued, “What I meant was, I don’t have any Johnny Mathis. But I do have something that might come close."

She stood, and Robert watched her hips sway as she slowly made her way to a small stereo. She kneeled on the floor, looked through the neatly stacked records, and selected a Kingston Trio album. The turntable clicked and the record dropped. When she stood, her skirt rode up her thigh a bit, and a song started playing.

“Scotch and soda, mud in your eye.”

She turned and walked toward Robert, took his wine from him, set it on the coffee table, held out her hand, and pulled him to his feet. The song continued,

“Baby, do I feel high, oh, me, oh, my. Do I feel high?”

Her right arm found its way to his back and she gently grabbed his hand with her other hand.

The song continued, “Dry martini, jigger of gin.”

His arm went around her. He was pleased that she wasn’t as tall with her shoes off, for it made him feel taller and more adult like. She pulled him closer as their feet moved very slowly across the teak flooring. The music seemed to fade in and out. The song continued, “Oh, what a spell you've got me in, oh, my. Do I feel high. People won't believe me. They'll think that I'm just braggin.”

She pulled him even closer and the song continued, “But I could feel the way I do and still be on the wagon.”

The closer they were together the more womanly she seemed. Her lips moved toward his ear and whispered, “That was nice Robert, but the song's been over for a few minutes.” How could that be he wondered? It seems like it just started.

Alexia said, “I’m glad that her boyfriend came.”

Robert said, “Her boyfriend?”

“Yeah, remember the young woman you were dancing with. I think you under estimated yourself. I’m sure she was feeling the same way I am right now." She looked into his eyes, and kissed his lips gently. He was shaking some and hoping she didn’t notice. Robert felt completely out of his league, but he wasn’t going to fight it. He wondered if this was a joke or a way to make him feel better or showing her appreciation for the walls. But when he looked into her eyes, they were moist and expressed an unmistakably honesty. She sighed and pressed her pelvic tightly against him and this time he made the movement for another kiss and she responded, as their mouths opened and the tips of their tongues met with very gentle slow movements. It seemed their tongues were gently stirring two irresistible liquids together that weren't difficult to mix, but the mixing had become so pleasurable they didn't want the process to end. Their bodies were pressed tightly against each other and she reached for his hand and led him into her bedroom. Again their lips sought each other. She unbuttoned his shirt and he slipped it off. She removed her sweater and turned around. He moved against her and unhooked her bra. She removed her bra and turned toward him. He pulled her to him and kissed her again, and they sat down the bed. She laid back and he gently took her breast in his mouth and moved between her spread legs. They must have both awaken at the same time and just laid there looking at each other. She smiled and took his hand and put it against her lips.

He said, "Do you remember when you said I'd be surprised what I could learn from you?"

She whispered, "Oh, God, I know. I do remember saying that, and at the time, I wished I hadn't said it, because it sounded like what you're thinking now." She smiled and continued. "Maybe I did mean that. I don't know. Guess it doesn't matter. Things just seemed to flow in this direction. It has been a long time since I've enjoyed being with somebody. I think it's about you being a real person. Well, that and you're very handsome." She kissed him and continued, "If I remember right, when I said that, I think we were talking about sardines."

Robert said, "Yeah, I guess. I don't really remember the sardine part."

She laughed and said, "Well, I'll say one thing, you're a quick learner. That was quite manly."

He said, "Thanks, but I couldn't have done it without you." She laughed and he continued, "And I could use a little more practice."

She laughed again and said, "I think you have it down pretty well, but we'll see. That reminds of something I read about that Scotch and Soda song. I read it a long time ago, so I'll probably mess the story up. The article said the Scotch and Soda song was a favorite of the Kingston Trio, even though it never got real high on the ratings. When they were going to sing the song one evening, Bob Shane, one of the Kingston Trio, had just come out on stage and was preparing to sing. He said, 'Could I have a sexy spot light, please?' One spotlight goes off, leaving one on him but shining less brightly. 'Could I have it a little sexier, please?' Both spotlights go off, leaving just the overhead lights. 'Could I have it just a little sexier?' Suddenly, all the lights go out. The audience went wild, clapping and screaming. Then Bob says, ‘Uh, not quite that sexy, please.’ With that, one spot comes on, hitting Bob perfectly on his crotch.”

Robert laughed and said, "You never told me why they stopped canning sardines?”

She said, “The canneries had been warned about over fishing Monterey Bay, and after thirty years of fishing, the sardines were gone. When people asked Doc. Rickets where the sardines went, he would always tell them, “They are all in the cans.”

Robert was on his back as she placed her head on his chest and then moved her naked body on top of his and straddled him and their mouths came together. Afterwards they were on their backs looking at the ceiling, “I love my new bedroom.” She put her index finger across his lips and said, "I like being with you. This is the most meaningful relationship that I've ever had and something that I'll never forget. Almost like your dancing with the real woman story. And I would hope that our relationship would be right up there with that milestone and not a hurtful relationship to remember but something very real and pleasant.” Her eyes were moist and she said, "Robert, I really do enjoy being with you and find you very attractive, but I don't think this is such a good idea to continue this kind of relationship. Not that I don't want to." She sniffed and continued, "And I suppose if I were selfish, I’d keep you for myself and I'd be with you as often as possible, but that's not me. I've learned a lot from being with you and you've brought me back to the person that I was before I stooped down to the level of that wealthy intellectual crowd. I need some friends that are not phonies. People like you. I just don't want you to get hurt over this."

He nodded and his eyes were moist and he kissed her and said, "I know. You'll find the right person. You deserve that.” Then he gently moved over on top of her and they came together again. Afterwards she had that smile that indicates she was thinking about something sort of funny that she wanted to keep to herself.

He said, “What?”

She said, “Oh, it’s nothing. I was just thinking. It’s sort of crude and kind of dumb. You don’t want to hear it.”

He said, “You have to tell me.”

She said, “Okay, I was thinking that you might have gotten a fuckin “C” in PE, but I have to give you an “A” in fuckin.”

He started laughing and finally said, “Oh, God, you were really listening to my whining. I would say that you moved to the top of my list of favorite teachers."

She laughed and said, "Who did I replace?"

He said, "Mrs. Randall, my piano teacher."

She said, "Well, I can’t match that because I don’t play the piano. Did she teach more than piano?"

He laughed and said, "No, I was only in the third grade."

She laughed and said, "That makes me feel better."

He said, "I think, for me anyway, this is one of those times that your grandfather was talking about."

She nods, kisses him and said, "Yes, for me too. I’ll never have a sexier window washer."

He smiled and hugged her, not wanting to stop being with her, but knowing it was the right choice.

Robert and Alexia Visit Dive Shop

They shower together, washing each others backs, prolonging the pleasure so as not to waste the time they have left, not really knowing if one or the other is thinking, why not continue this relationship. It would only take one of them to speak up, but neither spoke.

As Robert was drying her back and admiring her backside, he said, "Why don't we get some breakfast. I think there's a place up on Lighthouse."

She said, "Yeah there is. That’s a great idea."

They ate breakfast and Robert took Alexia a longer way home past the dive shop. Phillip, one of the owners, took on a shocked and confused look when he saw Alexia with Robert. Phillip was wondering how many girlfriends this guy had. And this was definitely no girl that he just entered the shop with. No, this was a woman. Robert saw Phillip’s expression, an expression that Robert didn't think possible from what he thought of as the most secure person alive. Phillip finally said, "You don't have tanks here do you?"

Robert said, "Oh, no, we're just in the neighborhood and decided to stop by. This is Alexia."

Phillip stumbling over his words, said, "I'm Phillip, You a diver too?"

She smiled and said, "Oh no, but it looks like a fascinating sport." They looked around the shop for a while. Alexia said, "These pictures are amazing."

Phillip said, "Well, I've been a few places, but you know, I don't think you can beat Monterey Bay. Maybe that's the one thing I've learned from traveling. This is where I want to stay." She nodded and smiled and Phillip waved as they walked out the door.

Alexia said, "What was that stop all about?"

Robert said, “I don't know. We just happened to be walking by. I just like looking at the stuff and he seems like neat guy."

She said, "Yeah, he does."

Robert said, "Ever thought about taking up diving."

She smiled and said, "Well, not until just now."

Robert laughed and put his arm around her and said, "You'll be okay, huh?"

She said, "Yeah, I think so. How about you? You gonna be okay?"

He smiled, "Yeah, I think so. But I'll never forget you."

She said, "I don't want you to forget me or what we had together. You know where I live. You can come over anytime. And I'd liked to meet the girl that I know you will find."

Robert's attention wasn't on driving as thoughts of the experience with Alexia raced through his mind. He was in a daze when he glanced into the rear view mirror and saw three cars close behind him. He looked down at his speedometer and saw that he was only going fifty-five, which was far too slow for this road. His mind seemed to be fogged over. He stepped on the accelerator and the Chevy slowly eased up to seventy. The Chevy cruised nicely at seventy, just took a while to get there, with the six cylinder engine and Powerglide transmission. The three cars behind him still wanted to go faster and eventually found safe places to pass him. He sighed and felt content, as he settled into being relieved, by the reduction of complexities that had entered his life. He started thinking that the time with Alexia could well be one of the most amazing times of his life and thinking of it should be a pleasant thought, rather than a hurtful thought. He wished he had left some tools at her place so he would have had a reason to go back. But he might go back and find someone else doing her windows. Sometimes he just wished he could turn his brain off, for he knew he was going to mentally obliterate himself by thinking stupid stuff. He said to himself, "I have a bad habit of over analyzing everything, and the complexity of my thinking does not match my attempt at simplicity."

He turned on the radio and it was in the middle of a Buddy Holly song, "Now you go your way baby and I'll go mine, Now and forever till the end of time, And I'll find somebody new and baby, We'll say we're through, And you won't matter anymore."

Weekend after Alexia

The following Saturday, Robert was moping around, missing Alexia and Nona and trying to figure a way to perhaps have a time share thing with both of them. But as pleasurable as the thought seemed, somehow he knew that would not end well, nor was it an option that either of them had offered. This missing somebody or needing somebody was new and very frightening, depressing, and all of the above. If a person had never tasted chocolate, they wouldn't miss it. And that was the problem. He had been handed an open box of premium chocolates, but others were eating out of the same box. He laughed at himself thinking that was quite a profound thought. He had to accept the fact that Alexia and Nona had not intended for him to have access to the whole box. They had merely passed him a sample piece because they felt sorry for him. Now, he was back to thinking he could call Lynnette, but since being with Nona and Alexia, he had entered a new realm where he had real feelings for somebody and a craving to be with them. And Lynnette obviously understood their lack of feelings for each other a long time ago. He had been going to the drive-in with Lynnette because it felt good physically without the complexity of an emotional attachment, similar to professional dancers that believe an emotional attachment with their partner might distract from their dancing skills. However, Lynnette was instrumental in sharpening his kissing skills and she seemed to enjoy teaching as much he did learning. The two of them were definitely in sync and seldom resorted to watching the movie. As he thought along these lines, the same logic could apply to his relationship with Jim and Gary. The three of them dive together, drink some beer, kid around, but there doesn't seem be a yearning to be with them. The attachment is diving. The attachment to Lynnette is making out, but they had no meaningful conversation with each other and the most that ever came out of their nightly romps was enhanced kissing skills and chapped lips. She had told him she learned kissing from her girlfriend. He thought that was okay and at the time, the thought occurred him to ask if her girlfriend could maybe give him some lessons. But, at least he was astute enough to keep his mouth shut. Yet as that thought shot through his mind, it seemed like it could have been interesting. When it came to relationships, he would have liked to think that he was beyond being stupid and could actually pick up on the obvious, say and do the right things, but he knew that was not yet within his grasp, nor was he sure it would ever be. His mind shot back to the third grade and Janet, the girl who wanted to trade sandwiches and it took him about seven years to figure out she made that sandwich herself. No, he never surprised himself with his high level of stupidity.

Conversation with Carl

He had worn himself out thinking and making an attempt at unraveling the knots of the twisted life that he had gotten himself into. It had been a couple weeks since he had seen Carl, so he gave him a call. Not for a date, but conversation. He was another friend that hadn't found his lifetime girlfriend yet, but Robert figured Carl was so confident that he didn't feel the need to dwell on it much. Carl grew up in Salinas and seemed to know everybody and everybody knew and liked him. Robert liked being with him because they had meaningful conversations. Though he was the same age as he and his diving buddies, Carl seemed more grown up and more intelligent than any of them and most assumed, and probably correctly, that he would become very successful. However smart and grownup Carl was, he did have one fault, for he wasn't old enough to buy beer either. But, fortunately they had a system in place to get beer, and generally if the two of them got together, having a beer or two or three was understood for it promoted conversations resulting in solutions to local and worldwide problems. Well, perhaps not, but they did have meaningful conversations with a beer or two. Robert also had another motive in getting together other than not being able to get a date. They cruised into Chinatown, an area off Market Street. Chinatown was initially inhabited by Chinese settlers that worked in the fields converting grazing land to very valuable farming land for the land owners, eventually giving Salinas the lettuce capital of the world title. At one time Salinas had the second largest Chinatown in California, slightly smaller than San Francisco's Chinatown. Neither of them had ever seen any Chinese in this area that now seemed to be a skid row. They were specifically looking for Hank, who generally hung out down there. They didn't know if that was his real name, but he answered to it and could always be counted on to buy beer for them. They spotted Hank, parked the car and walked down to him. They each gave him two dollars to get a six-pack of Coors and something for himself. They stood by and waited for him to come out of the liquor store and within five minutes he had an ice cold six-pack, a bottle of something in a brown bag, and a little over a dollar in change. He handed them the beer and money.

Carl said, "Keep the change, Hank."

Robert said, "Thanks, Hank."

Hank smiled and said in fatherly manner, "You boys be careful." Robert smiled, nodded, and thought he should bring that Blaine guy down here to learn some manners.

Most the under-age guys would go out on a country road to drink, but Carl and Robert generally parked on a side street off Main and watched the guys and gals drive in circles. Sort of like watching a drive-in movie, without the necking part, and it allowed them see a variety of cars and kids and at the same time save some money on gas. But with gas at fraction less than thirty cents a gallon you didn't save that much. And if you filled the tank, you might even get green stamps and or a set of glasses. But driving around in circles is not a relaxing way to enjoy a beer because you have to worry about rear ending another car or running over a pedestrian in the crosswalk. Probably the police wished that all the teenagers were drinking beer on the side streets instead of creating the drag Main Street traffic.

After a beer and some regular conversation, Robert, said, “Carl, you know Lynnette, right.”

Carl said, “Oh, yeah we started grade school together. Nice girl. You still going out with her?”

Robert said, “Well, not really. We weren’t clicking. I mean we did a lot of you know, drive-in time and that. But she started to not be available. I guess I didn’t pay enough attention to her or she just didn’t like me.”

Carl thought for a few seconds, nodded a couple times and said, “Well, you know, she’s always been a little different. I mean very nice, but I think she might have some gender issues.”

Robert, puzzled look, said, “Gender issues?”

He said, “Yeah, you know, maybe likes girls more than guys.”

Robert, concerned said, “God, Carl, you think I caused that?”

Carl, a very sober look said, “Well, you probably didn’t help it any.”

Robert still concerned, "Oh, don't tell me that Carl."

"No, you know, I've known her since grade school and she's always had that tendency, so most guys that grew up with her always treated her nice but sort of stayed away as far as asking her out and stuff. But you hadn't known her before and she is very nice and very pretty. I think you asking her out maybe threw her off track for a while. You might have been her first date. She did talk to me once about her situation. I just listened and learned. This was new to me too."

Robert said, "Yeah, well, she has a good friend that she seems real close to. I'm just not too familiar about girls like that because girls always seem close to each other. They can walk the street holding hands, dance together, have pajama parties and nobody thinks anything about it. But, two guys holding hands and pajama parties, well that's another story. You know one of my friends likes guys. I just didn't think about girls being that way."

Carl nodded and said, "Well, I'm sure it's not easy for anybody that has feelings for the same sex." When the beer was gone and a couple complex world problems solved, Carl dropped Robert at his car.

It was about midnight and Robert, still feeling sorry for himself, decided to do something that he had never done before and something that he would soon regret. Since Nona lived in North Salinas and he lived in South Salinas, it made absolutely no sense to drive past her house, particularly since it was well past midnight. It wasn't as though she would be waiting up for him. Not only that, since he had been drinking and fewer cars were on the streets, the police still might have ticket quotas to meet. He knew he was not a road hazard for he wasn't really drunk, but the problem with beer is that you drink just one and it marks your breath for the evening. He'd heard vodka didn't give you that alcohol breath, but he didn't know if that was true. As he drove north, he knew Nona and her parents would be sleeping, but he had no intention of stopping or anything and his inner voice continued to remind him that it would be a senseless trip. But, he was on his way, and no logic was going to stop him. And sure enough, as he traveled North Main, a few blocks ahead, a police car is parked on the side of the road. Robert thinks about taking a right turn on the next street but decided that would make them real curious, so he keeps going straight. He is going a bit over the speed limit, but backs off a little and his nondescript Chevy seemed to tip toe past the police car. Robert watches his rear view mirror knowing he'll see the red flashing lights. But now, quite a ways past the police car, he sighed and felt better. But what he would discover minutes later would be much more hurtful than getting a ticket or even being put in jail for the night. As he turned onto the street and approached Nona's house, he sees Chuck's car parked at the curb and the house was completely dark. Robert's mood went from bad to really bad.

Images started running through his mind. He had misjudged her. He wondered if the pajamas that he wore that night were actually Chucks. They did seem rather big. His mind raced with thoughts, unbearable thoughts. He couldn't imagine Fat Fuck Chuck being satisfied with simply snuggling. He knew that neither one of them were wearing anything right now. She had been just playing him like cheap guitar. He could imagine Nona telling her football groupies and whoring cheerleader friends, whatever they are, about the sissy whose handle is Commando Guy, a boring hick from Montana, who couldn't even get it up in bed. Telling them he was not man enough to go ahead and stick it in. And maybe that's what he was. Well, hell yes, he thought. That's what I am. I'm a stupid, boring hick from Montana. He saw her nipples sticking through her pajama top that night, but did he try anything? No, the only thing he knew to suck on was a scuba mouthpiece or a snorkel. What was he thinking that night he spent with her? What was he thinking? Did he think she would ask him to do her? Yeah, sure, he could picture her saying something like, "Excuse me, honey, but why don't you pull down my pajama bottoms and stick it in, instead of laying there like a stupid shit. And make damn sure you hit right hole. It's the one just past the belly button." How stupid he was. He started remembering how he couldn't even talk to Janet when he was fourteen years old without stammering. And not looking at the naked sister in that Saco bedroom was an obvious indicator that he would turn out a measly masturbator boy. Old Blaine was right on with that one. And at this very moment, Alexia is probably getting it doggy style from Butthead Blaine, while she's thinking about how long it took that sissy masturbator to get it on. He couldn't even count his time with Alexia, for she didn't really want to do him. It was a way to reimburse him for his loft work. And Lynnette, well, he made her a true believer in being a lifetime lover of girls. Not only all that, it's too late to go diving. Or maybe it's not. Maybe it's time for a Monastery Beach nitrogen narcosis journey.

Nona Calls

The next morning after not sleeping much at all, the phone rings. Robert picked it up and miserably said, "Hello?"

Nona cheerfully, "Hi."

Robert in a detached voice said, "Oh, hi."

"What's wrong? You seem kind of down."

Robert couldn't say anything about Chuck's car at her house because he didn't want her to think he was spying on her. He curtly said, "I'm okay. I'm okay, just tired."

Nona said, "Up for a beach walk?"

"I don't know." He hesitated for several seconds and finally said, "Yeah, I guess."

"You don't sound like you are."

"I'm just sort of, I don't know."

"I'll make some sandwiches and I have a special treat. And I have some news about Chuck and I." Now, Robert knew for sure that she had made plans to not see him anymore. Her and Chuck probably got engaged since they were sleeping together and Chuck knows how to do it and doesn't require an invitation or instructions and probably has a manly thing, being a big guy and all.

He said, "Why not tell me about Chuck now?"

"No, not on the phone."

He was very quiet as they drove to Monterey. She said, "I've never seen you like this before. What's wrong?"

"I'm fine. The visibility was crummy yesterday."

He pulled off the road at an isolated beach near Asilomar. There weren't many cars passing by and there wasn't anybody near the beach area because the fog rolling in made it very chilly, well actually cold, and the weather, though typical for Monterey, didn't help Robert's state of mind.

Nona said, "I brought the blanket. Would you bring your canvas to sit on?" Robert nodded and grabbed the canvas. They put on their sweaters and she handed him the blanket and grabbed a bag containing the sandwiches and another bag, containing drinks. They found an isolated beach area near some rocks, sat down on the canvas, and she covered both of them with the blanket. Then Nona looked at him very sternly and said, "Now, listen, tell me what's wrong." She waited and said, "What happened?" He sat there and wouldn't even make eye contact with her.

He finally looked at her, tears formed in his eyes and he starting sobbing. He quickly turned away and started wiping his eyes with his sleeve and said, "Oh, shit." Then he decided that he might as well tell her the truth because they were over anyway. "Well," He took a deep breath and continued, "I'd been with Carl last night and we drank a couple beers and talked. I left Carl about midnight and then did something real stupid."

She looked worried and said, "A drunk-driving ticket?" She paused, "Get in an accident? Hurt somebody?"

He shook his head said, "It's too dumb and I had no business doing it. I mean, what you do is your own business. He's your boyfriend. I'm just a dumb shit nobody."

She gets a very concerned look that is almost turning to anger, then tears form in her eyes, she softens and hugs him. "What do you mean? Why did you say that?"

"I did something dumb. I drove by your house on my way home. I'd never done that before. I don't spy on you. I mean I don't drive by your house. And I don't know why I did it. It was a stupid thing to do. And it wasn't any of my business." Robert started crying again, shook his head and said, "He's your boyfriend. It's none of my business what you do with him."

Nona realizes he saw Chuck's car in front of her house. She shook her head and pulled him into her arms and said, "Oh no. No."

He shook his head and said, "That's your boyfriend. You don't have to explain. I don't want to make trouble for you. I just have stop liking you so much. And I can do that. It will just take some time and… "

She hugged him tighter and said, "No, I want you to like me a lot." She gently pulled back from him a little and looked into eyes, "Chuck and I broke up last night. It's been coming on for a while. He wasn't in the house. Come on, now. Chuck's been drinking too much for a long time. Last night we were at a party and he was so drunk he was making out with another girl. And you know, I didn't even care, because I found somebody else too. I left him and drove his car home. So that's why his car was there. He came over this morning to get the car and I told him it was over."

Robert tried to rub the tears from his eyes and said, "Oh, God, I'm sorry. I just, I don't know why I acted like such a dope. Maybe because I am a dope."

She clinched her jaw, raised her eyebrows, smiled a little, and said, "Well that's a real possibility. But, I think you might be in love."

He said, "Is love that painful?"

"I've heard it can be."

He said, "I'm mad at myself for thinking bad things about you."

She said, "It's funny, I've always thought of imagination as a good thing. But I see how it can be destructive and override trust and logic. And I don't think imagination is always controllable. Let's put this behind us."

He said, "How can I be such weak crybaby."

She said, "There is nothing wrong with crying. It means you have feelings."

Nona grabbed the bag and pulled out two of the six the beers. "Chuck left this for us in his car, maybe it will help."

Robert, with his tear stained face, looked and nodded like a child that finally got its way, and said, "Well, it might."

Nona laughed, kissed him and said, "You're something else, you know that." They each took a long drink and breathed in the salty air. The ocean waves were crashing against the large rocks and then up onto the beach. Nona lay on her back and they kissed again and then rolled onto their sides facing each other.

Nona said, "What is it about the ocean? It's cold, violent and noisy, yet gives me the illusion of peacefulness."

Robert nodded, "I know what you mean. It's like watching a magnificent wild animal from a safe distance."

She said, "You know, if we didn't have an imagination and completely based our lives on reason and logic, I don't think we would be very interesting. And things might never be invented or created. I think imagination and love might be related because they are both intangible. Love can be heartbreaking or magnificent. Imagination can be amazing or tragic."

He nodded and said, "Wow, I hadn't thought about that. You know you're a very smart person."

She smiled and said, "Yeah, I know."

He laughed and continued, "You remind me of Carl, only you're a little prettier. You know Carl, right?"

She said, "Everybody knows Carl, but I don't think of myself as a smart person." She sighed and continued, "It seems like I could lay down here with you forever."

He said, "Maybe it's just that we aren't together long enough for you get tired of me."

She said, "I know what you mean but, well, I think there's more to it than that. But I don't want to over analyze it like some people do."

He nodded, smiled and said, "Yeah, I know the type. You know, I'm so glad you called me. I was going nuts."

"Well, someone had to make the call."

"Yeah, I'm sorry. This is like an early Christmas."

Nona smiled and said, "You know, my parents are away for the weekend again. Maybe you could keep me company tonight, but I don't think you'll be unwrapping any gifts."

"That's okay. I just like being with you and holding you."

She smiled and said, "I know. A person can't fake that. But it's nice to hear you say it."

He said, "Seems like your parents are away a lot."

"Well, my Mom's mother lives by herself and they visit her quite often to do things around her house. But they also think because I'm getting older and didn't go away to college, I need some separation from them to become more independent. A lot of my friend's parents hang onto them like they are still in junior high and don't seem to have the faith or trust that my parents have for me. To my parents, it's important that I become responsible and held accountable. And it's not easy for mom, because she likes being with me, but wise enough to know separation can also be a good thing for it seems to draw us closer together."

Robert looked at her, slowly nodded, and said, "I see how you got so smart."

She smiled and said, "Well, I admire them for thinking that way and it makes me try to maintain their trust by doing the right things. And that's not always easy, especially when I'm with you." She kissed him and said, "What about you and your parents?"

He said, "Never thought about. Seems like they always assumed we would do the right things. When were really young out playing on the streets at night, a lot of the kids had to be home at a certain time, but my brothers and I never had a certain time. We sort of picked our own time. We didn't have any rules. My older brother is the only one that seemed to take advantage of the freedom we had. And I think my younger brother and I saw how he took advantage of our parents and misused their trust. With his excessive drinking and car wrecks, he put my parents through a lot misery and expense that they couldn't afford. Maybe that's why my younger brother and I tried to do the right things. I guess we felt they had enough bad times with him. He never seemed to care about anybody but himself. And don't know why he was that way. I don't think I'll ever know. I'm sorry. I didn't mean to get off on this. You know, I've never told this to anyone before." Robert eyes were moist and he said, "I'm sorry."

Nona's eyes had become moist too, she hugged him and said, "It's okay. I've never had conversations like this either. When I'm with you, things seem to pour out. And I'm happy that you seem to respond the same way. What a perfect situation, someone that you can talk to and make love with." She wiped her eyes with her arm and continued, "Talking like this makes me want to lie down here, hold you tight and drift off to sleep."

He nods, but then takes on a confused look, "But, I keep wondering about something."

She said, "What's that?"

He said, "Well, when I am expected to be more aggressive? You know what I mean?"

She said, "So you want to know when to climb on, and do me?"

He shook his head, nervously laughed, and said, "No, I didn't mean like that."

She smiled and said, “Yes you did Commando Guy. That’s what you were trying to say but you tiptoed around, right?”

He nodded and said, “Boy you get right to the point, huh?”

She laughed and hugged and whispered in his ear, “Trust me, you’ll know. God I like being with you.” She paused and continued, “But do you think I'm using you?"

"I hadn't thought about it. But guess it's true."

Nona said, "Yeah, I know. But, don't you think we use and get used by people all the time."

He said, "That might be where the term reliance comes from. Maybe getting used is not a bad thing. I don’t mind you using me. I guess the deciding factor would be the motivation of the person that is using.”

Nona nodded and said, "Yeah that makes sense. You know, even though Chuck and I broke up, it doesn't mean we have to go together. I don't want to tie Commando Guy down."

Robert laughs and said, "That's a difficult handle to live up to anyway, especially when he’s crying like a damn baby. But what happens when you find out I'm just an ordinary boring guy?"

Nona said, "I don’t see an ordinary boring guy. I see a very honest and caring guy. And you know, there is something very manly and brave about a person being able to be themselves and having honest feelings and being able to cry.“

He said, “Well, I was sure was good at the crying part. I was wondering about something?”

She said, “What’s that?”

“Well, how did your Dad know I was from Montana? I don’t think I ever mentioned that to you.”

She said, “I was in your speech class.”

He said, "Oh, shit. You know I made all that stuff up, right?"

She laughed and said, "No, you're not that creative. It took me several days to stop feeling sorry for you. Oh, and speaking of my Dad, he said, when you spend the night you can help yourself to a couple of beers."

"Oh, shit, no. How did he find out?"

"I told him."

Robert, very upset, "Your Dad knows I sleep with you?"

"No he trusts you to stay with me because you're from Montana but knows you're in the spare bedroom. He doesn't trust you that much."

"But your Mom doesn't know about me staying there?"

"Oh, she knows and also knows when the spare bedroom has not been used."

He said, "Oh, no."

She smiled and said, "She trusts me enough to know that I will do the right things. And she knows that you respect me. She said she'd rather you stay with me than one of my whoring cheerleader friends."

He smiled, shook his head and repeated, "Whoring cheerleader friends." He then took on a very serious, puzzling look, and said, "What kind of beer does your Dad drink?"

She laughed, shook her head and said, "There you go, now see, that's a real manly question."

Chuck and Friends

The football team, being such an important part of any college, recruits the finest players from around the globe. Many of the team players have scholarships, which includes food, lodging and spending/beer money and the college even offers an education for the few that are interested.

Chuck and his two close friends, Leo and Bear live in a large, two story house close to the college rather than the dormitories. It's rumored Chuck was kicked out of the dormitories. It's about lunch time and Robert is getting into his car parked in the college parking lot. Chuck and his two large roommates approach him. Chuck gives a nod upward and says, "Hey Montana, this your car?"

Robert looks up and said, "Yeah."

Chuck said, "A piece of shit, huh, Bear?"

"Bear, whose nickname is self explanatory when he grunts, "Yeah, man."

The other gentleman, Leonard, whose nickname is Leo, not because of his first name, but because he snorts like a lion when he waddles down the field with his fat thighs rubbing against each other said, "Well, it matches this pipsqueak who drives it."

Bear grunts, "Yeah, man."

Chuck said, "Hear you been hanging around my girl." Robert ignored him and continued getting into his car when Chuck grabbed his arm. Robert squinted and stared at him and Chuck continued, "I just wanted to let you know that I was through with that little slut anyway. In fact, a couple days ago she came over begging for my big guy. I was busy doing this other girl so my buddies here, took care of her, you know kept her warm, until I could get to her. Right, guys?"

Bear nods and grunts, "Oh, yeah, we kept her motor running."

Robert continues getting into his car and Chuck said, "So, what do you think of that you pathetic little shit?"

Robert said, "I'll think, I have to think about it."

Chuck said, "Well, chicken shit, you tell that slut if she misses sucking a real dick then I might consider taking her back. Not full time. Just when she needs that overused pussy reamed out, cause I doubt you're taking care of it."

The three of them watch Robert drive away, and Chuck said, "What a chicken shit. Jesus Christ, what a damn waste of a human being."

Bear grunts, "Yeah, a real sissy."

As the sun was going down Robert comes out of his house wearing an old army surplus jacket with large pockets and heavy hunting boots, carrying his Model 94 Winchester, a box of ammunition, and an army surplus bag hanging from his shoulder, all of which he puts into the Chevy's trunk. It's getting a little darker now as pulls along the curb near the rooming house where Chuck and his two friends live. He gets out of the car, opens the trunk and puts the strap of the army surplus bag around his neck. Then he takes the rifle out, opens the box of ammunition, loads six rounds into the empty magazine, and puts six more in his jacket pocket. He walks up the steps to the rooming house, looks in the window and doesn't see anybody, so he tries the door and it's not locked so he quietly goes on in. There is nobody in the kitchen and large area downstairs, but he hears voices upstairs. He walks up the stairs to a door and can hear Chuck and his buddies and a loud television. He could have merely turned the knob and opened the door, but he steps back raises his right heavy boot, and gives the door a strong kick. Chuck and his two buddies, sitting on the couch watching television and drinking beer, are stunned when they hear the loud bang and watch the door fly open along with the spray of wood splinters from the door frame and metal pieces from the latching mechanism and hinges. And then they see Robert standing in the doorway with a rifle. Robert was as impressed with the kick, as the bastards were surprised with the door flying open.

Chuck jumps up and yells, "What the fuck you doing? Oh, God, that's a replica. That's not a real gun." Then he smiles, spits out a little laugh, and continued, "Shit man, you had me going there for a second, asshole. That's a hell of a Halloween getup."

Robert casually jacked a round into the chamber, pointed the rifle down and shot a hole through the floor. The blast was louder than Robert had expected, but how was he to know, he had never shot a rifle inside a building before. He jacked the empty cartridge out and it hit the floor sounding like a symbol crash, marking the grand finale of the rifle blast.

He looks down and sees the front of Chuck's pants getting wet. Robert gently released the cocked hammer.

Leo said, "Jesus Christ man, we was just messing with you the other day."

Robert said, "Apparently, you should be more careful about who you mess with."

Bear said, "Yeah, man. Yeah, yeah, we can do that. We'll be real careful."

Robert said, "First, refresh me about Nona coming over here the other night. Which one of you started warming her up, you know, keeping her motor running, while Chucky was busy with the other girl?"

Leo said, "Oh, God, no, that didn't happen. You know, we were just messing with ya."

Robert squinted, shook his head very slowly and sternly said, "No, you weren't just messing with me, you were pissing me off. And it makes me wonder how often you pull this shit with people's lives. You know, I shot my first buck mule deer with this rifle when I was twelve years old. But you know what, I'll always feel worse about shooting that deer than shooting you assholes. Now, which of you started warming her up?" They sat speechless. Robert continued, "Well, guess it doesn't matter, but don't blame me if I start with the wrong one. And Chucky, don't worry, I'm saving you for last because I want you to see what's coming as you watch your two friends drop."

Chuck nervously said, "You're crazy."

Robert made an evil smile and said, "Well, maybe you should have thought about that before you fucked with me. You're probably not real good with statistics, but if you fuck with enough people, and I'm sure you have, then the law of averages says you're eventually going to come across a real nut job."

"Now, everybody take off your clothes."

Chuck crying and said, 'No, look my dad is wealthy. I can get him to buy you a brand new car. Any car you want. I know you don't have much money. I was in your speech class for God's sake. Just sat a couple rows from you."

Robert said, "No, I don't take anything. I earn things. My car is worth much more to me than any new car because I bought it myself with money I earned. A person that doesn't earn things doesn't deserve them. And Chuck, a person like you will never deserve anything you get because all you do is take. You don't earn anything. You're a slave to your pimp liberal father who controls your life like the government liberals control poor people by giving them welfare, food stamps, and cheese. These gifts keep the poor in place, never allowing them to feel the satisfaction of earning their own way and developing a sense of pride, and they actually believe the government is helping them. I feel sorry and respect those people, but I have no sorrow or respect for somebody like you." Robert waited for the unintended political lecture to sink in, and then said, "Oh, and you were also in my psychology class when you treated Doctor Healy badly. So part of this session is for Doctor Healy's revenge."

Chuck sniffling, "I was just messing with him."

Robert pointed the rifle barrel at Chuck's crotch and angrily said, "God Damnit Chuck, shut up and take your clothes off. And do it now. You're irritating me, getting on my nerves. You're gonna make me start with you, just to shut you up."

All three guys are naked and sitting on the couch together. Robert looks at Chuck's crotch, shakes his head with a disgusted look, and said, "Is that what you call a big guy?" Robert takes a movie camera out of his army surplus bag and said, "I need a camera man. Any volunteers?"

Chuck waves his hand as though he's in a classroom and the same time is shaking and crying, sniffs and said, "Yeah, I'll do that. Yeah, I can do that."

Robert said, "No, you'll be busy. You're gonna be my leading man in my entire production."

Robert has Leo stand up to shoot the action and said, “Chuck, do your thing on your pal.”

Chuck said, “Come on, this isn’t funny anymore.”

Robert sticks the side of the rifle barrel, that is still little warm, against Chuck’s cheek and the clicking of the hammer being pulled back seemed louder than the empty cartridge that had just hit the floor, motivating Chuck to go to work on Bear. Robert didn’t really expect Chuck to put it in his mouth, but the camera would assume that was what he was doing and maybe he was. He couldn’t really tell from where he stood. Robert said, “Now, Leo, sit down. Bear, take the camera.” Robert almost has to laugh because he doesn’t see any hope that Leo’s thing will ever come to life out of the mass of curly red hair, but Chuck puts his head down there and at least gives that impression, as Bear captures the action.

“Okay now, everybody to the bedroom. I need two of you on the bed for the sixty nine shots. But don’t fret; you’ll each get a turn.” Chuck starts to get up. “No, Chuck you’re our star. You’re in every scene.” With the sixty nine shots finished, Robert said, “Okay, see everybody got a turn.” He takes the camera, puts it back in the bag, hooks the bag on his shoulder, and said, “Everybody move out to the couch and sit down.” The naked three, move into the little television area and sit together on the couch, shivering and crying. Robert raises the rifle and briefly scans the barrel across the three of them to the end of the couch, pulls the hammer back, points the barrel down and shoots another hole through the floor. And in all honesty, he didn’t intend to do what he did next, but he went ahead anyway and jacked another round into the chamber, aimed the rifle and blasted the screen of the loud television set. Robert said, “That was for Doctor Healy. Okay gang, it’s been swell. Listen, if you guys want copies of this, it’ll be two hundred fifty bucks each. Make a great a Christmas present for your proud families who root for you every weekend, rain or shine as you perform your foreplay by chasing those guys around the field until you wear them down enough that they allow you to pat their asses. And I can only imagine what goes on in the locker room later. Gee, maybe I’ll come and visit you fellows there sometime. Oh, and I might give the girl’s sorority, a complimentary copy of the movie. Be great for pajama parties.

Anybody give Nona or me any trouble, the movie will become a real hit at the student store."

Robert put his rifle, the bag and the camera in the trunk and drove away thinking that he should have some regret, but just couldn't seem to work up any. And that bothered him. Maybe he was nuts. Pointing a loaded rifle at a person and shooting holes through a floor didn't seem to be real normal. Then he did feel a tinge of guilt because he realized he enjoyed the caper.

The next day Robert was on the phone, "Jim, I'm going to return your movie camera if you're going to be home."

Jim said, "Sounds good. I still don't know why you needed a busted movie camera. You could have used my good one."

Scuba Diving Monastery Beach

Two scuba divers, down about twenty five feet are making their way slowly through the kelp forest and two other scuba divers, who are holding hands, are about ten feet behind the leaders. The four divers find a clear area and group together. The unknown fourth diver pulls out a slate, writes something, and shows it to Robert. The slate said, "Love you."

Jim and Gary close in to look at the slate. They both smile nod, and make the OK sign with their fingers. Then Jim writes on his slate, "There go your Saturdays."

Nona moves close to Robert and removes her regulator mouthpiece and mask and Robert does the same. The two of them kiss.

Gary writes, "Looks like it'll be worth it."

Jim's hobby has always been photography, so it was a natural progression for him to take up underwater photography as well. He has them reenact the kiss. And as the two of them, again without air and masks, are thinking he was taking a long to snap the picture, finally see the flash.

An Unexpected Meeting

It's getting dark as Robert is leaving the college library and headed for his car in the parking lot. The parking lot has a few lights, but it's still quite dark and Robert sees a person approaching. It looks like a guy, but he can't quite make him out until he gets closer and then he becomes very concerned, because it's Chuck. He hadn't seen Chuck or his buddies since their get-together. Not that he had been looking for them. Chuck gives a nod upward and says, "Hey Montana, I like your car?"

Robert looks at him suspiciously and said, "Oh Yeah."

Chuck said, "Yeah, I'll never forget your 52 Chevy. And you know, if I can find one when I earn the money, I'm gonna get one."

Robert is very wary of the situation and suspects that Chuck is faking the nice guy thing hoping to get back the movie, or beating him up or some type of revenge said, "Why's that?"

Chuck said, "Because it will remind me of the only person that ever stood up to me. Can I talk to you? Maybe go get a beer? I know place on Market that'll serve us."

Robert was in a tight spot, for he figured Chuck's friends were not far away, but he really didn't seem to have a choice, so thought it best he take his car which would give him more control of the situation if things went bad, so he said, "Sure hop in."

As he started out of the parking lot, sure enough, another car pulled out ahead of him. He knew they might try to block him so he turned his car around and said, "Chuck, I forgot to get a book I need in the library."

Chuck smiled and calmly said, "Sure no problem. The bar don't close till two." Five minutes later Robert causally walks out of the library and gets back into his car. As they drive, Robert constantly has his eye in the rear view mirror. They pull into Maria's Tavern parking lot off Market, and go inside. There's an older couple at a small table and about four guys and a rough looking woman at the bar. The woman has an unfiltered Camel hanging from her lip with a decent ash on it. She kind of looks like she could handle herself in a fistfight with a man or woman, and it wouldn't even ruin her night or interrupt her beer. A woman bartender in her early forties, good shape and attractive, approached, smiled and said, "What you boys have?" Robert was concerned that she would ask for an ID but she didn't bring it up. Though he did have wine with Alexia in the restaurant that night, this would be his first drink in a real bar. And he figured it would be neat to be able come in once in a while for beer. Chuck said, "A draft for me, Maria."

Robert said, "Sounds good."

They each drank their mugs down about a quarter when Chuck finally said, "You know, you are the only person in my entire life that has ever convinced me that I am a rotten, fuckin asshole." Robert was in the middle of a taking a long sip of beer and nearly snorted it up his nose. But he didn't say anything. They drank their mugs down another quarter and Chuck's eyes seemed to be fogged over a bit and continued,. "Ever since first grade, I've been a trouble maker and by second grade, I was a full fledged bully. I was able to continue doing bad shit because my father knew that anything I did wasn't my fault. It was the school, the teachers, the principal. It was their fault I misbehaved. And my father, being wealthy, donated a lot of money to the school and he was, and still is, an overbearing asshole, that none of the school staff would go up against."

They finished their first draft, Chuck got Maria's eye and she brought two more. Chuck continued, "My mother tried to reason with my father, but he was a very powerful person both mentally and physically. And early on, I discovered I didn't even have to listen to her because anything I did around home was not my fault. And my mother eventually just gave up on me."

He drank about a quarter more of the beer and continued, "When I asked Nona out the first time…" Chuck hesitated and tears started forming, then he sniffed, and continued, "I was shocked that she said yes. She was the first girl that I ever respected and I knew that I didn't deserve her. But being with her was like I had become the prom king and it made me proud. And I tried to be so careful around her because she was so special and so beautiful." Chuck started crying, he wiped his eyes, got up and went to men's room and washed his face and came back, and said, "Sorry."

Robert placed his hand on Chuck's shoulder and said, "Chuck, it's okay."

Chuck continued, "It took me weeks to just kiss her and we never did do that very much. She was almost more of a friend than a girl friend. And I was okay with that. I was so proud to be seen with her. But, I wasn't a different person unless she was around. So, I was actually just acting, maybe trying to change, but it wasn't working, even though I wished it would have. I just want you to know that nothing ever happened between us. But I'm sure you know that." Both mugs are empty. Robert catches Maria's eye, confidently puts up two fingers like he knows what he's doing and Maria nods.

Chuck said, "Montana, what you did that night was the gutsiest thing that I've ever seen in my entire life. I keep thinking that if I were a soldier on the battlefield, I'd want you next to me." Chuck started crying again shook his head and said, "Shit."

Maria came over, and with a very concerned look said, "Chuck, are you okay?" Chuck looks at Maria and nods. She hands him a clean bar towel and said, "Here, hang onto this, Honey."

Chuck looked at Maria in very loving way started sobbing again and said, "Maria, nobody has ever called me that before."

Maria looked puzzled and said, "You mean Chuck?"

Chuck, tears still streaming, shook his head and said, "No, I mean Honey."

Now, Maria's eyes were moist, and she came around from behind the bar, gently grabbed his shoulders, turned the barstool, pulled him to his feet and hugged him for about a minute. Chuck melted against her like it was the first real or honest hug that he had ever experienced, and Maria, feeling his tears on her cheek whispered, "It's okay honey. It's going to be okay."

More composed and again back in his bar stool, Chuck said, "Montana, you taught more that night than my father, the schools, the coaches, or anybody that has ever tried to intervene. You taught me something that I had never understood. You taught me humility by the most dirt awful humiliation anyone could dream up. But, initially, the lesson didn't sink in and I tried to figure a way to get back at you, but then I began to realize what you did was just what I needed. You taught me that if I didn't get my shit together and break from my father's hold I would never be a happy person." Chuck started crying some but continued, "You taught me I'd better start earning my own way or I'd continue down the road with faked pride. And I realized that part of the reason I was such a jerk was because I have never been a happy person, not even a happy little kid, because I have no real pride. Everything you did and said was so true and of course, perhaps more convincing since none of us really thought we were gonna get out there alive. We didn't know you. The only thing we knew about you was that we pulled your hammer back and you let us have it with both barrels. We thought you were a nut job. I doubt that I'll ever be that afraid again. You know, I haven't done anything to patch the holes in the floors or even replaced the television set. And door is still hanging by a couple screws. I need that damage to remind me."

Robert held up two more fingers, and Chuck said, "Montana what do you know about the fishing out of Alaska?"

Robert puzzled with the question, said, "Well, I know it's hard work and dangerous but pays well I guess."

Chuck said, "Well, I'm going to quit college and go there and work the fishing boats. A while back, I read a book a fishing boat captain wrote. He described the difficult life on an Alaskan fishing boat. He said each time he went to sea, he would take pictures of the crew, put together a scrap book for each cruise and keep notes of each crewmember. He said he needed to keep track of which crew members were reliable enough to come back from a night on the town and which ones were not. He needed every crewmember when they went to sea, so if they had a history not coming back, he would lock them up on the boat when they were in port to offload fish. He was showing his wife one of his scrapbooks and after she finished thumbing through it and seeing the pictures of the crew, she had a worried look on her face and said, ‘These are not human beings. These are animals.’ So, I think if I’m working with animals like myself, it might further motivate me to become a better person because I’ll be able to see myself through those guys. And I’ll be able to earn and save my own money and not rely on my father. I’ll be able to buy my own 52 Chevy. Oh, and you’ll be glad to know, that I’m no longer a damn liberal like my father. I know I’ve been doing too much talking but that night you kicked open our door, started me on mission to be a better person. I’m not suggesting you become a motivational speaker. I don’t know if everyone would respond to a Winchester like I did.”

Robert laughed and said, “You a catholic?”

Chuck, shook his head with a puzzled look and said, “No, I’m not, not much of anything, but sure not a catholic.”

Robert said, “Oh, just curious. Hey, you wanta drive a 52 Chevy, to get the feel of it?”

Chuck gets a big smile and in all sincerity said, “Really? You’ll let me drive? Hey, Montana, I just thought of something. You know I was in your speech class and I thought maybe when I get back from Alaska, you and I could pay a visit to that guy that said you lived in a shitty house.”

Robert laughed, and said, “Oh, he’s taken care of. He’s on my list.”

Chuck, with a puzzled look, said, “Your list?”

“Yeah, I have a list of people whose graves I’m gonna piss on.”

Chuck said, “No kidding. Hey, did I make that list?”

“No, you didn’t Chuck. You didn’t piss me off bad enough. You just irritated me a bit.”

Chuck laughed, shook head and said, “Jesus.”

Robert smiled and said, “You know, Chuck, you’re going to turn into a nice person.” More tears started flowing from Chuck’s eyes.

The two of them got up and Maria said, “Where you guys going?”

Chuck said, "Oh, he's taking me to pick up my car."

She said, "Chuck, do you live by yourself?"

He said, "Yeah, right now I do."

She said, "I want you to come back after you pick up your car and help me help lock up. I don't want you to be by yourself tonight. And, I don't feel like being by myself either," then she raised her eyebrows and continued, "Okay?"

The Dive Shop

A few weeks later, Nona and Robert are in her bed. Nona is smiling as she looks over at the nightstand next to the bed. She's looking at a framed picture of her and Robert kissing in the kelp forest of Monastery Beach. She said, "About ready to get up? We're going to take the tanks over, right." He nods.

As they were driving down the Monterey Highway, Nona said, "Do you know something about Chuck quitting school and going to Alaska?"

He said, "A while back he approached me about going for a beer."

She said, "That must have been a little scary."

He said, "Yeah, at first I thought he was going beat me or something, but we went over to Maria's Tavern, sat the bar and had a nice discussion. He talked about going to Alaska and working on the fishing boats. I didn't mention it because I didn't know if he was serious."

She said, "I was sitting in the student lounge, and he came over and apologized for treating me badly and said he was quitting school and going to Alaska. He just seemed different. Nicer, I guess and happier. I heard he even went over and apologized to Doctor Healy for something he said in class a while back. He seemed quite impressed with you and said you were a keeper."

Robert smiled and said, “Are you sure he didn’t say I was kept man?” Nona nodded and smiled.

They get out of the Chevy and open the trunk containing four scuba tanks. He picks up two of the tanks and Nona picks up the other two and they carry them inside the dive shop. Robert looks toward the counter and gets a very surprised look on his face. There is a woman behind the counter standing next to Phillip. The woman waves and smiles at Robert and he waves back. They set the tanks down in the charging area and walk to the counter.

Robert smiles and said, "Alexia, what are you doing here?"

Alexia said, "Phillip says I have to work Saturdays to pay for my diving lessons." Phillip put his arm around Alexia. She looked up at him and smiles.

Alexia comes out from behind the counter, hugs Robert and said, "I'm so happy."

He smiles and said, "I can see that."

"Well, that too, but what I mean is, I'm happy for you." She looked at Nona, smiled, and continued loud enough for Nona to hear, "I can tell that you found the perfect girl"

Robert nods, looks at Nona and smiles and then said, "Nona, this is Alexia, an old of friend of mine."

Alexia laughs and said, "I'm not that old."

Nona smiles, takes Alexia's hand, and while still holding it said, "Nice to meet you, Alexia. When you finish your lessons maybe we could have a girl dive day.”

Alexia smiles and gives Nona a long hug, "Yeah, I'd like that."

Nona said, “You live in Monterey?”

Alexia, while still hugging said, “Well, Pacific Grove. I have a loft in an old cannery on Cannery Row.”

Nona said, “Oh, my gosh, it sounds so historical, so romantic.”

Alexia said, “So, you’ve read Steinbeck’s, Cannery Row.”

Nona eases back from the hug a little, looks Alexia in the eyes, nods and said, "Oh yes, I love that book. I wish I knew more of the cannery history and about the people that worked there."

Alexia smiled and said, "I'm sure we could learn a lot from each other. Maybe you and Robert could spend a weekend sometime."

Nona excitedly, “Oh yes, that would be really special, huh Robert?”

He thinks for a couple seconds, nods and said, “It might be real interesting.”

Unexpected Call

Mahogany bookshelves line the walls of the room. One corner has eight leather chairs in a semicircle surrounding a leather topped mahogany table and an elegant large mahogany desk sits in the middle of the large library-like room. It’s the kind of room you might see in a movie where the men leave the women at the dinner table, go off and smoke cigars, drink scotch, and try to impress each other. Blaine, Alexia’s ex-boyfriend, looking like he hasn’t shaved in several days is sitting at the desk in his robe. A half bottle of scotch is sitting near him and he is holding a tall glass in one hand and a telephone in the other. Blaine quietly and hesitantly said, “Is this Robert Murray?”

“Yes it is.”

“Robert, this is Blaine, Alexandria’s friend. Do you remember me?”

Robert, irritated said, “How did you get my number?”

Blaine, in an apologetic manner, “Well, I know some people at Hartnell. They gave it to me.”

“What do you want?”

"I wondered if I could talk with you."

"About what?"

"I'm thinking about killing myself."

Robert thought about saying okay, but instead said, "Why?"

"I guess because I don't have any friends. I know a lot of people but have no friends."

"Why call me?"

"I don't really know. Maybe to apologize for the things I said. Would it be possible to meet with you?"

Robert, suspiciously said, "No, I don't think so."

Blaine, sounding genuinely pathetic said, "Okay, I'm sorry to bother you. I shouldn't have."

Robert started realizing that Blaine might actually be serious about killing himself, and quickly said, "Wait. I'll meet you at Maria's Tavern tomorrow about eight. It's off Market Street in Salinas."

"A tavern?"

"Yeah, a tavern."

He said, "Okay. Yeah, I'll be there."

It was close to eight as Robert drove toward the tavern, still thinking there was a possibility that Blaine might not show. He sounded somewhat drunk and maybe after he sobered up he changed his mind about meeting. He wished he had made their rendezvous earlier because it was starting to get dark and there was also a chance that Blaine was trying to get some kind of revenge. As he pulled into the tavern parking lot he spotted Blaine's car and saw he was still sitting in it. He pulled up along side him. Blaine waved and got out and didn't seem to have any kind of weapon, so he got out and without saying anything, they shook hands and head inside the tavern.

Maria said, "Oh, Robert, haven't seen you for a while."

"Yeah, been busy diving, working and school. Maria, this is Blaine, he's from Monterey"

Maria smiled, shook his hand, hanging onto it a little longer than you might expect, but maybe because he was a new customer, said warmly, "Very nice to meet you Blaine. What can I bring you guys?"

Robert said, "A draft please, Maria."

Blaine looked at him funny and said, "Beer? Draft beer? I don't normally drink beer."

Robert said, "I believe beer promotes realistic down to earth solutions to problems, whereas other alcoholic drinks promote philosophical BS." Blaine surprised Robert by laughing and that seemed to break some of the ice between them.

Blaine nods and said, "You know you could be right. I'll have a draft too, Maria."

They sat looking at the row of liquor and decorations behind bar without saying much of anything until they both finished their beer and ordered another. Robert finally said, "I still don't understand why you picked me to call?"

Blaine shook his head and said, "I'm not sure. Maybe because I felt I should apologize for the things I said, and I certainly do apologize. And also I thought it would help me talk to you because Alexandria spoke highly of your honesty and character. I guess I thought you could somehow help me become a more likeable person because you would be honest with me."

"Why not get a psychologist?"

Blaine smiled and shook his head and said, "I have one. And I've been seeing those guys for years and the only thing they convinced me of is that they are as screwed up as I am."

Robert laughed and held up two fingers. Maria nodded and brought two more. Then Robert said, “Blaine, maybe your problem is that you didn’t have the luxury of growing up poor.”

Blaine, with a puzzling look, “What?”

Robert said, “When you have everything handed to you with no struggle, you don’t develop pride or self worth. And without pride, you can’t be happy because when you obtain wealth without earning it, you have no sense of accomplishment. And apparently your education accomplishments, which are quite impressive, aren’t enough for you. Maybe if you’d paid your way through college by working at a real job in a fast food restaurant, then it might have made a difference.”

Blaine gets in a stupor for several minutes, nods and said, “You know, that makes sense, but I can’t change that.”

Robert said, “Maybe it’s not too late to give a try. Maybe scale back your life style. Get rid of that pretentious car and get a Chevy or Ford and start living on your professor’s salary rather than relying on and flaunting your wealth. Try to find out who you really are, rather than that person you hide behind. Start hanging around some real people that aren’t pretending to be more important than they are. People like the ones that come in here. Most that come in here don’t come to impress anyone.”

Blaine nods and slurring his words said, “Maria, would you mind if I came in here once in a while to learn how to be a nicer person?”

Maria said, “Honey, you can come in here whenever you want. You’re not driving back to Monterey tonight, are you?” She raised her eyebrows, smiled and walked down to serve another customer.

Robert looks at Blaine and said, “Looks like you already have a new real friend.”

Blaine nods, smiles and said, “Yeah, She seems really nice. Pretty too, huh?”

“Yes she is, and they don’t come any better than her. You gonna be okay Blaine?”

He nods and said, “Yeah, I think so. Thanks for meeting with me.”

Robert said, “Well, you have my number and I’ll meet you here anytime. It doesn’t even have to be an emergency.”

Blaine nods and said, “Thank you. That means a lot to me.”

Robert leaves Blaine at the Tavern in Maria’s hands, and as he drives toward home, nods his head and said out loud, “Oh, to have had the advantage of growing up without wealth.”

THE END

About the Author:

Glen Watson was born in Glasgow, Montana and moved to Salinas, California as teenager. He spent many hours scuba diving in Monterey Bay. He later joined the United States Navy, where he became a submariner, serving aboard diesel and nuclear fast attack submarines. Recently, he has come full circle and now lives in Bigfork, Montana with his wife Marg, two dogs, and two horses.

www.ingramcontent.com/pod-product-compliance
Lightning Source LLC
Chambersburg PA
CBHW061216170626
46809CB00003B/1380

* 9 7 8 0 6 1 5 6 3 3 7 3 2 *